book one of the Seers Series

The
Guardians
of Eastgate

Happy Reading!

Sherry Leclerc

Sherry Leclerc

book one of the Seers Series

The Guardians of Eastgate

TERNIAS PUBLISHING

TERNIAS PUBLISHING

http://terniaspublishing.com

(© 2018) Cover art, cover design, map illustration, interior formatting, epub coding, and editing by Aidana WillowRaven

ISBN (paperback): 978-1-7751345-0-3
ISBN (hardcover): 978-1-7751345-1-0
ISBN (epub): 978-1-7751345-2-7
ISBN (pdf): 978-1-7751345-3-4

Dedication

For my mother, who has always been my greatest supporter. She encouraged me throughout her life, and she continues to inspire me every day.

Table of Contents

Part I:
Preparations

The air is thick around me with the stench of smoke and dust,
But I find myself surrounded by those I know and trust.
We have gathered all together to stand against our foe,
Who seeks to bring an end to the life we've come to know.

Fire blazes in the distance and the sounds of battle ring
As we watch the people rally to the hope our presence brings.
Adding to our strength as they gather to our side,
Our numbers shake the earth; our foes tremble, run and hide.

Our allies start to cheer aloud; they think we've won the day,
But through the cinders and the ashes a lone figure makes his way.
He moves along in silence, power crackles in the air,
I feel his presence calling, "Approach me if you dare!"

Raising up a glowing hand, I feel his threat to strike.
Yet he holds no weapon: neither sword nor knife nor pike.
My beloved stands beside me, but his face is out of sight,
And as I move before him, my eyes open to the light.

STERRENVAR

Thuaidh
Mountain

Dorcha Lake

The
Dark
Woods

○CS

N

Division Woo

BS

Foraoise Nao
(Sacred Fores

Fair
Harbor

WG ◉

GC

Fores
Lak

Hope
Bay

Fairwood

CS

DS

S

Cruache Mountain

Southwood

Fuar Point

Northwood

Forest Glen

Shichan Lake

EG

Peace Harbor

Eastwood

mad Mountains

Legend:

WS= Wolf Shifters
ES= Eagle Shifters
BS= Bear Shifters
DS= Dragon Shifters
CS= Cougar Shifters
NG= Northgate
EG= Eastgate
SG= Southgate
WG= Westgate
GG= Great Gate
▦ = Farmland
AM= Anwyl's Mine
◎ = Keystone Keep,
Castle & Castletown
⛰ = Mountains
🌲 = Forests/Woods

Chapter 1

Maelona awoke with a start. Her heart pounded in her chest, she was soaked with sweat, and her breathing was quick and heavy. When the dream left and the fogginess cleared, she found herself looking up at the bright stars in the dark sky through the circular opening in the roof of her hut. She did not remember all the details of her dream-vision, but she felt as though she was on the verge of panic. She took a few deep breaths and focused on one bright star shining above her to try and push past the anxiety. "Let it go," she said to herself.

This was far from her first dream-vision. She should be used to it by now.

Maelona thought about the dream-visions she'd been having regularly over the past few months. Actually, it had been years, but they did not come very often in the beginning, and she hadn't understood what they meant. They had become more frequent as time went on, however. Despite not knowing all the details, she knew that something big was going to happen soon. Something dark and insidious was threatening the realm and would leave it forever changed. It was yet to be seen whether this would be for the better or for the worse.

There were still many uncertainties, but one thing she was sure of was that she would do everything in her power to ensure it changed for the better.

Maelona rose from her bed and stretched, to try and loosen some tension. She moved over to her basin of water to splash her hands and face, then she dressed in the pale moonlight that filtered in from the roof and windows of her hut. She took her time; one thing she had learned about herself over the years was that calm actions helped to calm her mind.

She was quiet and calm still as she made her way to the gathering place. This was a large, covered, wooden structure where her people, the seers, came together to discuss matters of importance. She remembered many meetings where strategy was developed on how to gather information and, when necessary, to respond to threats that endangered the balance of the world or the future of the people in it.

These meetings were never taken lightly, and tonight's gathering promised to be one of the most important in centuries. When Maelona thought about this, and about her part in what was to come, she had to take a couple of deep breaths again. She went through the teachings of her father in her mind again to bolster her courage.

As a child, her father had explained to her the core of the seers' belief system: because of their particular gifts, the seers considered themselves guardians of the realm. They believed wholeheartedly that they were gifted their abilities by the universe so they can protect the realm and all the beings in it. This was the reason why they were created and placed in the realm. To do this, they sought to investigate and infiltrate any new threats to the people of the realm. As much as possible, they acted from the shadows in unobtrusive ways.

Just as evil can be insidious, her father had explained, polluting the good of the world with many small, seemingly insignificant acts, the solemn oath of the seers was to be the antithesis of this darkness. Their job was to remove evil when possible and bring light to the darkness in ways unseen by most. Only rarely, in cases of extreme threat and danger, did they play a larger, more visible part in the world. Maelona's instincts told her this was one of those times.

The remembrance of her father's convictions, his strength, and his goodness was the only thing that gave Maelona the strength to face what was to come. To do what he would have done. After all, it was her duty and responsibility to honor his memory.

Tonight, Maelona knew, only the seer elder and champions would be meeting together here. She entered the gathering place and Kelwyn, the seer elder and leader, greeted her.

"Maelona Sima," he said with a nod of his head, as was the custom.

"Kelwyn Kunagnos," she returned with a nod of her own.

Kelwyn greeted the three other seer champions as they entered the gathering place after her. Maelona nodded to each of them with the reverence and respect that came from many years of working by their sides.

Maelona knew many dangers lay ahead for all of them, and the foreboding feeling from her dream still lingered. She knew the entire realm was in danger, and none more so than herself and her fellow champions. She did not know what the future held for them, so she allowed herself the time to really look at her friends as they entered.

Talwyn Sevi, at six feet two inches tall, was about three inches taller than Maelona. Talwyn was tall and lean, with flaming red hair that traveled down to the middle of her back in a tumble of waves. She was fierce and fearless with a sarcastic wit that never failed to amuse. In other words, she was as fiery as her hair. Maelona held back a small smile at this thought.

She had first met Talwyn as a child but did not see her again for many years. When they did meet again, however, there was an instant bond. Talwyn looked out for her as if she were Maelona's big sister. In fact, Talwyn had taken to calling her "little sister" over the years. Maelona worried for her friend now. The battles to come would be harrowing, and Talwyn had already endured so much loss in her life.

Edan Carr entered right behind Talwyn. He was six feet six inches of lean muscle, with an intimidating presence but a mischievous and fun-loving demeanor. Out of her three comrades-in-arms, Edan had been the hardest to get to know. He kept a lot of things buried under his happy-go-lucky façade.

Maelona let out a huff of amusement at this thought.

Perhaps she and Edan weren't so different in that way. They both had much turmoil swirling under the surface. He disguised his demons under a humorous and light veneer. Maelona's veneer was calmer; seemingly unaffected and neutral. She was quiet and tended to listen more than to speak, while Edan was more boisterous and outgoing. While they might outwardly seem very different, they were essentially doing the same thing for the same reason.

The last champion to enter the room was Eavan Elestren. At five feet seven inches, she was the most petite of the group. Her physical stature and friendly, unassuming ways had in the past led many to underestimate her intelligence, competence, and martial art skills. She was a force of nature, both in her skills as a fighter and in her capacity for compassion and the care of others. Yet she was also very humble and modest.

They were all so different, yet Maelona knew they would all give their lives to protect the realm, without hesitation. They each brought their own unique strengths and talents, and together they had become one of the most formidable and successful teams of champions in the people's history. Given what was coming their way, Maelona hoped this was the universe's way of ensuring that good would overcome the insurgence of evil that threatened the realm. While the future was far from determined, she was glad she had these three on her team.

Maelona had managed to become close with the others over the years, and she would trust them with her life. Yet, she hadn't let them in, not really. She found herself regretting that, now that she knew the possibilities of what was to come.

Once the greetings were out of the way, Kelwyn addressed the group. "You all know what has brought us here tonight, and you know that since we are all here together, we have all had visions. We know that the present danger affects not only our village and people: the future of the entire realm is at stake."

Kelwyn then turned to Maelona and said, "Would you like to share your dream with the others, Maelona?"

Maelona nodded and began to speak. "I saw us gathered together, fighting demonkin in a town that was nothing but fire and ruin. We were able to rescue many, but many other villagers were injured or killed. We were accompanied by many allies…"

"Well, that's good, right?" Edan interrupted.

"Of course, but my dream-vision didn't end there," Maelona said. "We had many allies, and we had managed to fight back the demonkin horde. Just when we were ready to cheer our victory, however, a figure stalked out from between two burnt-out huts. There was smoke everywhere, and he was partially hidden at first. As he walked forward, however, I still couldn't see his face. It was shadowed and unclear, hidden inside his cowl."

"Do you think this could mean he is someone we know?" Talwyn asked. All four champions looked to Kelwyn.

"It is possible," he replied. "I am not convinced that is the case, though. There are too many things that have been blurred from our sight. Too many holes in our visions. Yet, these holes are all to do with the being behind the coming destruction. It is as if there is a powerful sorcerer blocking us."

"Is that even possible?" Talwyn asked.

"If the being was powerful enough, then yes," Kelwyn said.

"If this were a person," Eavan said, "he or she would have to be immensely powerful to do such a thing on such a large scale."

"Indeed," Kelwyn confirmed.

"Maybe we should stay out of this one," Edan said. "Stay hidden in the forest. It's not like the humans, or any of the others, have ever appreciated it when we've put our lives on the line for them."

"I hope you're joking," Talwyn said.

"Of course I am," Edan responded. "About the not helping, anyway. The part about them not appreciating our sacrifices is true. Otherwise, our race would not have been vilified the way it was."

"Did you see anything else?" Kelwyn now asked Maelona.

"Yes," she replied. "And it supports your theory about a powerful sorcerer.

"In my dream-vision, the male figure came from between the huts, as I said, and as he came closer, he raised his hand. It was glowing brightly, as if he were holding a ball of blue light.

Just as it seemed he was about to attack, I awoke."

Everyone was silent as they thought about the implications of Maelona's dream-vision.

After some time, Kelwyn spoke again. "For the past three hundred years, since our kind was mercilessly hunted to near extinction, we had hidden ourselves away and ventured out of the safety of our valley only when our people were directly or indirectly threatened. Whenever we interacted with the outside, it was from the shadows, for the good of our own people and for the good of the realm of Sterrenvar.

"As seer champions, you have trained and prepared for the eventuality of this night. Tonight, we embark upon a journey that will take us outside of the safety and shelter of anonymity. However, we all know we cannot turn our backs. Our entire world will be threatened: our way of life, our culture, and those we care for deeply. It may take more time for the evils that are about to be unleashed to seep through the deep forests and find their way to our humble village, but the world is a living organism, and what affects one, affects us all. Make no mistake, we will feel it."

Kelwyn paused for a moment before continuing. "This may be the last time we are together for some time, and you all need to be as prepared as possible for what is to come.

"You must each travel to your gate towns. You must gather allies along the way to support us at the Great Gate. If we are right about this sorcerer and his power, we will need all the help we can get.

"While you will be traveling separately, each with your own job to do, do not forget that you are all pieces of the whole. You each will need to complete your tasks if we are to be successful in bringing the realm through the dark times that are upon us. Keep each other up to date whenever possible." With this last, he looked to Maelona meaningfully, and she nodded to him in acknowledgment.

Though the champions already knew many details of what was now being set in motion, Kelwyn had a charisma and an aura of wisdom that always helped to inspire and encourage the people of the valley. And of course, it didn't hurt that the seer champions never had to explain their dream-visions to him. He always saw everything they saw, and often with more clarity and understanding.

They shared much knowledge between them and understood their role in the realm. Yet, Maelona could not remember even one time when Kelwyn failed to give a motivational speech when the opportunity presented itself.

When Kelwyn finished speaking, Maelona approached him.

"I know you think it is just part of your responsibilities as our elder, Kelwyn, but I would like to thank you for the guidance you have given us in figuring out what we were seeing these past few months. Without you to bring all the broken images together, we may not have been able to see what was coming until it was too late."

"There are still plenty of uncertainties, young one," Kelwyn said. "Stay alert and aware out there. It has never before happened that one has been able to block our visions to this degree. Whoever is behind the coming darkness is powerful indeed."

Yes, there were many uncertainties, like whether she was ready for what was expected of her or not. But Maelona was certain of one thing: she would do everything she could to succeed. She would put her own life on the line if she needed to. After all, it was the least she could do.

She could single-handedly save the entire realm, and it still would not erase the dark spot from her soul - the only thing she never told her seer friends about.

As the sun was rising over the horizon the next day, Maelona headed out, knowing there was one stop she had to make along the way. She walked toward what would be the bustling center of the village later in the day and made her way to the smithy.

As she approached, a familiar face came into view, and she smiled fondly.

"Anwyl Govan," she greeted him.

"Maelona Sima, my anum cara," he replied. "I am so glad you came to see me before leaving."

"You know I would not leave without seeing you first, Anwyl. I will miss you while I am gone, and would take your image with me on my travels."

Maelona looked at her soul friend and noticed the strain of emotion there. But then he cleared his throat and moved to retrieve a large wrapped parcel on a back table.

"I made these for your birthday, but as it seems you will not be here at that time, I thought it would be fitting to give them to you now."

Maelona took the package gently from his hands and placed it on the bench in front of her before pulling back the cloth that was wrapped around it. What she saw was a set of daggers, six throwing knives, and a short sword the like of which she had never seen before.

Finally, there was a copy of her favorite weapon, rendered in this new metal. It was a cylinder about a foot long, and she knew if she pushed one button, it would extend to about four feet long. Another button push, and it would extend to six feet.

She put the extendable staff into a holster at her lower back and lifted the daggers up. She turned them in her hands, feeling the weight and balance of them as they glinted in the early morning light.

"These are exquisite, Anwyl. They must have taken you some time to forge."

"I have been working on them since my return from the Cruache Mountains. The metal in your blades was found there. The tribes that live in the mountains call it galanite. It is much stronger and lighter than any other metal I have worked with, and I thought it would be perfect for these gifts for you. I had actually completed them last week, and it would seem the timing is perfect, since you now have need of them sooner than expected."

Maelona had learned soon after arriving in this village as an adolescent that Anwyl was the village blacksmith and the best metallurgist the people had known in a few centuries. As Maelona looked over each of the weapons, getting the feel of them and admiring the workmanship, she knew she would not find weapons of such high quality and reliability anywhere else.

She felt a little tug of emotion as she thought that carrying these weapons would be like carrying a piece of her heart with her through the coming journey and struggles.

Maelona began switching out the weapons in her leather holsters with the new, higher quality weapons. Then she turned to her friend and said, "I shall carry them with me always, Anwyl, and care for them as if they were part of myself."

With that, they embraced warmly, and then Maelona turned and headed out of the village.

Maelona was just reaching the edge of the village when she heard a voice call out behind her.

"Maelona! Wait!" Talwyn jogged to catch up with her.

Maelona smiled warmly at her good friend. "Talwyn Sevi. Coming to say goodbye?"

"No, little sister," Talwyn replied. "I am coming to remind you that you are not alone." Talwyn grabbed Maelona by the shoulders and looked her directly in the eyes. "You can count on us. You know this, right?"

"Of course," Maelona said.

"Then *allow* yourself to rely on us, Maelona. Don't bear everything by yourself. I will try to sleep as often as I can so my mind can be open for you."

"I really appreciate that, Talwyn." Maelona said, fighting to keep her eyes from watering. Maelona knew that Talwyn was plagued by horrible nightmares, so her offer to sleep often was a very significant show of support.

"I promise I will check in when I can," Maelona said.

"Good," Talwyn replied. "I will see you again at the Great Gate in a few weeks time. Take care of yourself, little sister."

Maelona reached out and embraced her friend. "And you as well, big sister. I will see you soon."

With that, Maelona turned and headed away from the village once again.

She climbed a narrow pathway that led up the steep embankment out of the valley. When she reached the top, she looked back over the village. From here, she could barely see the little huts dotted about, hidden under the canopy of trees below.

This is the place she had called home for more than half of her life. These people were her people. And they were good people. All they wanted to do was take care of the realm, even when the people of the realm turned their backs on them. Even when those people hunted them.

Now she wondered if she would ever see the Valley of Sight again and, if so, would it be the same?

Chapter 2

The wolf watched from the underbrush where the forest gave way to the grassy bank of the lake as the dark haired, dark eyed female stripped down to her linen undergarments. He probably should have left to go hunt at that point and given her privacy. However, after shadowing her for more than a week, he found himself becoming more and more curious about her, wanting to learn more about her before making his presence known. And, he had to admit to himself, he found himself becoming strangely protective of this female trekking through the woods alone.

As he looked at her form now, though, with more flesh bared than he had seen thus far, he couldn't help but think that maybe there was more to her than first meets the eye. This thought was sparked by the lean yet well-defined musculature now visible along her legs, arms and back. He had never seen a female so well muscled before, even though his pack had many strong females. She looked strong but still distinctly female. He liked this more than he would have expected.

The female scrubbed her clothing against a rock. When she seemed satisfied with their cleanliness, she laid them on a flat rock at the edge of the water to dry. She unwound her hair, which had been braided and twisted up elaborately so that it was tight to her head. As she undid the intricate work and shook out her hair, he realized it was much longer than he expected, coming down almost to her waist. She then proceeded to bathe herself before diving into the water.

She was submerged for some time, and when she finally re-emerged and walked to the edge of the lake, she was carrying a large fish skewered on a dagger. *Strange*, he thought, *I hadn't noticed a dagger before she dove in.*

Yes, definitely more than meets the eye.

The wolf continued to watch her throughout the afternoon as she started a fire, cleaned and cooked the fish, turned her clothes over on the rock, ate the fish, and then proceeded to clean and sharpen the dagger she had used to catch and clean her dinner. Then, testing the dryness of her clothing and seeming satisfied, she proceeded to dress.

She wore pants made of supple leather that were laced all the way up the sides with leather ties. Her shirt was also of the same leather and laced down the center. She then crisscrossed two leather straps across her body. There were several small knives in each of these. She tucked her two daggers into the straps at the front of her chest, handles facing down. In one of the straps where it crossed over her lower back, she put a cylindrical object into another holder. Finally, she added a small pack to her back, with a strap that crossed from shoulder to waist and a second strap that attached around her waist.

She did not seem in a hurry to move, but the wolf was not surprised by this. In the week that he had been shadowing her, she had slept only twice. Each time was between supper time, when she lit her fires and cooked while there was still daylight, until a couple of hours after nightfall. The rest of the time, day and night, she was moving at a pace that was efficient, but which he suspected was almost leisurely for her since she never appeared winded at all.

Because her present activities seemed to be maintenance activities, and because she hadn't slept in a couple of evenings, he suspected she would tonight. *Thank the heavens*, he thought. He was one of the stronger of his people and had excellent endurance, but he suspected he needed to sleep more often than she did.

The sun started to lower on the horizon, painting the sky in reds and oranges above the treeline. The female sat upon the same large rock she had dried her clothing on and then started to braid and twist her hair again as she looked out over the still water of the lake toward the sunset.

So quietly that he wasn't sure what it was at first, she began to sing. It was not a language he was familiar with, but as she sang her voice grew in strength, and the intricate melody began to flow smoothly. It had an almost hypnotic quality to it, and the wolf found himself laying down in the brush and closing his eyes, allowing the sound to wash over him.

A couple of hours later, he startled awake to the darkness of nightfall. The only light was from the moon, which shone full overhead. He sat up and looked toward the lake, trying to see the female. His animal sight made it rather easy to see at night, and he was sure after looking around that she was no longer there. He was lifting his nose to scent the air when he froze at a low voice coming from behind him.

"I see you wolf."

He turned around to see the female sitting with her back against a tree a couple of feet from him, shadowed from the moonlight by the branches above. She had her arms wrapped around her knees and was leaning slightly forward, capturing him in her keen gaze.

"I bet you thought you were watching me all this time. Really, we were watching each other. I know why you think you are here, but I don't need a protector or an escort, wolf. I could use a partner, however. I warn you, though, my journeys will be long and dangerous. They are also necessary to the safety of the realm. If this is something you might be interested in, come find me as the sun rises."

At this, she stood and disappeared into the trees.

In the pale light of dawn the next morning, the wolf walked out from the brush toward a small fire, where the female was sitting, eating a breakfast of fish from yesterday's catch. He approached slowly and cautiously, a bit wary since the revelations of last night.

As he got close and sat across the fire from her, he carefully took in her features, and what he found surprised him. As he had watched her from a distance this past week or so, and then again last night in moonlight and shadow, she looked almost plain, someone who would not stand out in a crowd. But from close-up in the light of early morning, he was surprised to see that her features were striking. She had dark brown hair and warm brown eyes, and her face was smooth skin and soft, feminine angles. She was beautiful.

How is it that I have been following her for more than a week, but these last two days have revealed more than all the previous ones combined? He wondered to himself. But then the thought suddenly occurred to him that maybe it was because she had allowed it.

Maelona leisurely took in the impressive, large black wolf. His ice blue eyes were striking, and seemed familiar to her some-how. "I know what you are, wolf, and I know why you think you are here. The sorceress sent you out with the task of escorting me in and protecting me, but she did not tell you why. She merely told you where to cross my path."

When he gave a little jump, she continued, "Do not be so surprised. I am a seer after all."

Well, that explains a lot, he thought.

"Like I said to you last night, I do not need to be protected. However, given the seriousness and the difficulty of my task, I would be grateful for another set of ears and eyes - and let's not forget the nose in your case as well," she added. The corner of her mouth lifted in the slightest of smiles.

"I neither expect you nor want you to make a final decision until you know exactly what you are in for," she continued. "But since we both trust the Sorceress, and we've spent the last nine days watching one another, I think a sign of faith might be good at this point. I gave you my sign when I approached you last night. Now it's your turn. Show yourself, wolf."

Maelona watched as the male shifted from wolf to human form, his shape shimmering as if it were a mirage, moving from four great paws to two thick, strong legs. As he stood, Maelona stood as well, so that when he was finally standing tall, and he lifted his head, she only had to tilt her head up a little to meet his eyes.

When Maelona saw his eyes this time, as he stood as a man in front of her, she felt a jolt of surprise that made her lose control for just a split second. His jet-black hair and ice blue eyes matched his wolf coloring. But now, she recognized them from many hazy dreams, mere flashes of blue in a sea of onyx, in visions with no context that she could recall. She had an idea of what that meant. He was strikingly handsome, with a strong, square jaw and dark, thick eyebrows that made his eyes stand out even more.

She took him in even further, letting her gaze fall over his tanned skin and then continue down over his tall and well muscled form. His human form was one that would leave an impression on any who saw him.

Finally remembering herself, she inclined her head toward him and gave him her name.

"I am Maelona Sima."

Inclining his head to her in return he simply said, "Blaez."

Her mouth curved into a small smile as she said, "We still have much travel ahead of us, and I would like to get to your village as soon as possible. Let's head out."

"Should I be surprised that you know where our village is?" He asked.

"The knowledge that I am a seer should answer that question for you," she replied.

Over the next few days, Blaez came to understand how much he missed from his 'secret' surveillance of her. Now that they were traveling together, Maelona was revealing much more about herself and her capabilities. It was as if she had decided she could trust him and dropped her guard, at least to a degree. He could tell that she was trying to hold herself aloof; trying to hide the deeper parts of herself.

Every morning, Maelona climbed to the top of the tallest

nearby tree to scan the horizon and, at first, Blaez was surprised by her balance and agility. He also found himself feeling a little surprised at the speed at which Maelona seemed capable of travelling for extended periods of time.

"You know, your speed and the way you move so gracefully and noiselessly through the forest remind me of my own people," he commented one afternoon. Instead of responding, she just looked at him and smiled.

He did not know much about seers, as they tended to keep mostly to themselves after being nearly exterminated a couple of centuries ago, according to local lore.

"Do our peoples have a lot in common?" He asked. She looked at him quizzically, and he added, "I get the feeling you know more about my people than I do about yours."

"You would be right about that," Maelona replied. "And, yes, we do have a lot in common."

Blaez waited expectantly for an explanation. However, one never came. He let it drop for the time being and hoped that she would open up as she got to know him better.

Blaez often found himself staring at Maelona as they travelled, but he didn't always realize he was doing it until Maelona caught him watching. Then, she would look over at him with a small smirk. This made him think, or worry, that she could somehow tell what was on his mind at any given moment.

Before long, Blaez realized that Maelona was a quiet person. She seemed to spend a lot of time wrapped up in her own thoughts or examining the forest around her. He also realized that this was just her nature. She wasn't intentionally cold. He knew this because, from time to time as they walked and hunted together, he would touch her or brush against her. Every time that happened, he felt a warm, tingly sensation where their flesh met. He knew she felt this too, because whenever they touched, her cheeks warmed pink with blush. And whenever that happened, he found himself thinking, *so beautiful.*

She never once pulled away. They had only just met but already he knew, he was lost for her.

One day, when they were still a few days out from his village, they had slowed down to track small game. They moved carefully and quietly across the forest floor. When she looked over and grinned slightly yet again, he found himself unable to hold his curiosity for any longer.

"Tell me, Maelona, I do not know much about your people, but I do know there is a good reason you are called seers. What is it you do? I have heard you get visions. Is it the future you see? Do your visions always come to pass?"

"We do get visions of a sort," Maelona replied. "Our visions can be of the past, present or future. Usually, it is easy to tell which, though sometimes time itself seems to lose all meaning. And no, our visions do not always come to pass, thankfully. If that were the case, then it would be pointless for us to try and intervene, to guide things in the direction of good. Sometimes, though, those involved may be so intent on their goals, so focused on the actions they have decided upon, that nothing could change the outcome."

"Are these visions the extent of what you can do, or is there more?" Blaez inquired. "Some years ago, for example, I heard rumors that your people can see into the minds of others. Is there truth to this?"

"No," she responded. "At least, not in the way that you mean. It is not the mind we read. Rather, it is a person's physical cues. We are so attuned to our own physical bodies that reading what lies behind others' physical reactions is easy for us. And then we also train this ability from an early age. It is a person's words and tone of voice. It is their facial expressions, their body language. These things can often be subtle, but they sometimes stand out as if they were begging to be noticed."

Blaez found himself feeling a little nervous about what she may have read from him in those times he thought himself inconspicuous as he watched her. "And myself? Do you find me easy to read?"

"You have been a male of very few words…until today that is. Now you seem to have endless questions." Maelona smiled and glanced over at him as she spoke. "You have generally been very calm and steady. Even this unassuming way you have about you says a lot. Also, your eyes are very expressive. They have many stories to tell, and even more questions than you have given voice to." She said this with a glint in her eyes and a smirk on her lips.

"A person's eyes speak the loudest as to who they are on the inside," she explained. "And there you have the reason why I am answering so many of your questions after only knowing you a short time.

"Now, let's get back to what we were doing. More hunting, less chatter…you're going to frighten all the game away with your constant questioning."

With that, they continued their path in a comfortable silence.

That evening Maelona and Blaez shared a stew of rabbit meat and roots and tubers they managed to dig up along the way. They had finished their meal, cleaned up, and put out the fire just as dusk was coming fully upon them. Now they sat in companionable silence upon a ridge where they were camping out for the night, watching the moonlight dance among the tops of the trees.

Blaez thought back over the last few days. The kinship and easy rapport he had developed with Maelona over this short span of time amazed him. Never had such a thing happened to him before. They hunted and foraged in tandem, each seeming to innately understand the others' actions and intentions. They moved quietly: it seemed that no words were necessary between them.

He supposed this was normal for Maelona, given what she had told him about her people. But even though his own people often hunted in packs, this level of comfort and understanding was new to him. He marveled at how this had come to pass, even though they barely knew anything about one another.

Blaez lay back in the grass and looked up at the stars dancing above them. "Tell me more about your people," he said.

"I supposed it's only fair since I know much more about your people than you do about mine." Blaez turned his head to see her smiling down at him. Before he could ask her what she meant, she continued.

"I told you before that we read a person's physical cues. But there is a lot more we do, as well.

"We also watch, and we study the people and cultures in our world. Seers are even more long-lived than your people, and that gives us plenty of time to watch and learn. Usually from a distance, but sometimes joining with different groups, assimilating their ways and blending with the culture. This gives us the opportunity to learn things that outsiders would normally not be privy to."

"Doesn't that give you a kind of power and control over others? Are you not worried about some of your people being tempted to abuse such power?" He asked.

Maelona gave him a wry smile, and he could see sadness in her eyes. "We are protectors of balance and light. We do not long for power and control, not in the way you mean anyway. It is not in our makeup. And even if there were one among us who would be tempted by such things, my people learned long ago that we are not infallible. By showing our abilities too openly in the past, we left ourselves open to the kind of fear and suspicion that led to people worrying about that exact question. And that led to our kind being hunted down and slaughtered.

"So, for the past few centuries, we have gotten involved only when our visions have shown that the safety and security of entire peoples or our entire realm was in danger, either in the short or long run. And we have taken care to act from the shadows, never revealing ourselves openly. Sometimes it can be as subtle as influencing someone to make the right decision when they otherwise may have made a wrong one."

Blaez looked at her with a questioning furrow on his brow. "If you have such powerful visions and so much knowledge, then how is it that your people could not avoid being hunted and slaughtered?"

Maelona could read on his face that he was simply trying to understand, and she believed he could be trusted. So, she would give him the information he needed to be able to trust in her as well.

"Well," she answered, "one interesting thing about my

people is that we do not get clear visions of things that will affect us personally. We may get a sense of things that will affect us, but no one of us can see our own fates. It is our blind spot, so to speak. Even so, the elders at the time knew there was something evil brewing, but they did not know the exact nature of the threat or how it would begin until the chain reaction had begun.

"Also, many of the seer people believed in letting the humans make their own decisions and mistakes and not interfering. After the attacks began, many of my people began having visions as well as learning in other ways that, even though *we* decided not to interfere with the humans, there were others who did not have the same consideration. In fact, it was discovered that evil forces were acting behind the scenes, fear-mongering and manipulating the humans into believing that we were a danger that needed to be destroyed. Our elders then decided that we needed to intervene, to stop these evil forces from destroying the peace of our realm.

"But, by then, it was too late to stop what had been put into motion," she added quietly.

Blaez looked out over the landscape for a moment before turning back to her. "Are the rest of your people like you? You seem resilient, like someone who could take care of herself. Did your people not fight back?"

"Like I said before," Maelona replied, "we are protectors. For the most part, our attackers were people whose fear and insecurities were being used against them. Most of my people refused to fight back against innocents who were being manipulated like puppets on a string, by evils that hid like cowards in the background. And, because of who we are, what we do, we tend to have a better understanding, respect, and appreciation than most for other cultures, as well as points of view that differ from our own."

Maelona looked away, but not before Blaez saw the sadness in her expression. "We eventually found peace again, but not before many innocent lives were lost."

"Can it really be called peace, though," Blaez asked softly, "if you had to hide yourselves away and deny your very existence to get it?"

Maelona looked at Blaez thoughtfully for a moment before turning her gaze upward once more to watch the clouds move in to hide the moon.

Chapter 3

The next morning when Blaez awoke, Maelona was no longer at their camp. He followed her scent until he broke through the underbrush on the bank of a small lake. Looking out over the water, he saw her a short distance out, floating in the water facing away from him. Without thinking twice, he stepped into the water. He swam out to where she was drifting and looking up into the clear blue skies.

As he swam toward her, without moving or looking back in his direction, she acknowledged his presence by asking, "So what's your story, Blaez? Why did the sorceress choose you to send to me?"

"Surely you must know the answer to that better than myself," he answered with a smile.

Maelona moved until she was treading water facing him. "I have seen you before, but usually only in flashes. I know your face, your eyes, your smile, your wolf, but that is all. Do you know what these flashes tell me?"

He had an idea, but he waited for her to continue.

"They tell me, Blaez, that you will be an important part of my future. You will become too close to me personally for me to see more than blurred images, general feelings, and the picture of your face the first time we met. I do not yet know the nature of our connection, and I am sure by the surprise I see on your face right now that you know no more than I do."

"I know only what Ailla Melyonen has told me," Blaez

responded. "I was instructed to meet you and escort you to our village, and to provide protection along the way."

"The sorceress always acts with a purpose. She knows very well that I know my way to the village and that I do not need protection. But since you only live in the shadowed corners of my mind, I do not yet know her reasoning."

"I work with her sometimes when help is needed. Maybe she believed you need my help," Blaez surmised.

"Well, she would most certainly be correct if that's the case." After a pause, she added, "You work with her, yet, you aren't a sorcerer, are you?" It was more a statement than a question.

Blaez chuckled and said, "No, not at all. She helped me out when no one else would. Now, we help each other whenever we can."

Blaez watched as Maelona's expression turned sad for a moment. Then, just as quickly, it cleared again.

"I don't know if you will be very eager to extend your help to me once you learn the nature of my mission. And before I can tell you that, we need to go see the sorceress."

At that, Maelona started swimming back to shore. Blaez turned to follow her, and as he looked in her direction, he found himself once again admiring the strong yet feminine shape of her form.

Due to the shifters' divergent physical nature, it was not uncommon for males and females alike to be naked or barely clad in front of one another. As such, he had seen plenty of examples of the female form. Still, hers stood out amongst the others he had seen, with both feminine curves and firm and developed musculature that made him think that she must have partaken in her fair share of hard work. And as he left the water and noticed Maelona eyeing his form appreciatively in return, he fought back a smile. He could not help but feel a sense of gratification to receive such a look from a female such as Maelona.

A few days later, they walked silently through the forest at an almost leisurely pace, tracking prey. Maelona placed her hand gently on Blaez's forearm as she slowed to a stop. When Blaez looked to catch her eye, she kept focused ahead and lifted her chin to point out something that had caught her attention. Blaez followed her gaze with his own, and ahead, through the foliage and into the clearing beyond, there stood a magnificent stag.

Up to this point, they had kept to small prey - enough to keep them fed, but not so much that they would be burdened with carrying the meat around with them for long periods of time. Blaez had noticed that Maelona liked to use as much of the animals they hunted as possible, with as little waste as possible. Since they were less than a half a day out from his village, he knew her intentions with this hunt. They would bring the meat to share with others in the village.

Since they were off to the side from the direction the deer was facing and slightly downwind, Blaez knew their scents would not give them away. Maelona signaled to Blaez to hide in the undergrowth behind the stag, and upwind. He marveled again at how silently she moved as she hid in the underbrush and disappeared out of sight. Then, he also moved silently through the ground cover into the place she had indicated. He removed his clothing along the way, as silently as possible.

A few moments later, his attention was caught by a light glinting from the bushes almost diagonally across the clearing from where he stood. With his shifter-heightened sight, he barely made out Maelona waiting a couple of hundred meters in front and to the left of the stag. She signaled him using the light of the sun reflecting off a blade.

Shifting silently to wolf form as he approached, Blaez headed to the rear of the stag. Lifting his nose in the air, the stag startled at the earthy scent of wolf in the air and bolted toward where Maelona lay hidden. Blaez took up the chase. Once in range of Maelona's hiding spot, Blaez leaped into the air, landing on the stag's haunches at the same moment that Maelona burst forth at a dead run toward them. Leaping into the air, Maelona propelled herself toward the stag's shoulders.

Blaez twisted his body so that his movement and Maelona's attack brought the animal to the ground on its side, where

Maelona quickly dispatched it with her knife directly through the heart. Blaez could not help but sit back and take a moment to replay Maelona's attack in his mind. She had moved faster, leaped farther, and displayed more efficiency and grace than he had ever seen before. *She would make a fearsome opponent, or a formidable ally*, he thought.

Blaez shifted back to human form, and he and Maelona began the cleaning and initial preparations of the carcass. As they worked, thoughts and questions began swirling through his mind.

"Do your people hunt together as mine do?" he asked Maelona.

"From time to time," Maelona responded. "But usually I hunt alone. It was nice to have a partner," she added with a smile.

"I have to say, you seem very familiar with my people and our ways. And you know the way to our village. Have you spent much time there?"

"I did, in my youth."

"Why don't I remember seeing you around?"

"There are many possible answers to that. For example, you haven't asked how old I am. I may have been there and back before you were even born. Or maybe we were just unlucky, and were never in the same place at the same time. Also, sometimes people change a lot as they age. Maybe I just look a lot different than I did when I was younger."

"You know which one of those scenarios is correct, don't you?" he said.

Maelona paused what she was doing and looked up at him. She considered him for a moment, as if she were deciding whether or not to answer. Finally, she stood up.

"I'm going to go gather what I need to make a sleigh to pull the carcass to the village," she said. Then, she turned and walked out of the clearing and back into the forest.

In the early afternoon of that same day, they arrived at Blaez's village with Maelona dragging the deer carcass behind her. For this purpose, she had made a sleigh of branches formed into a frame, crisscrossed and secured with vines from the forest and ropes from her pack.

From the time they had begun hauling the deer to the time that they arrived at the village, Maelona had become more and more quiet and serious. Blaez sensed that he shouldn't push, so he left her to her thoughts. He had hoped she would decide to talk to him about whatever was on her mind, but she did not.

Why are you so disappointed? He asked himself. *You haven't known each other very long. It's to be expected.* Yet he couldn't deny that it saddened him to see her pull back from whatever it was they had forming between them. Now he regretted pushing her with too many questions.

Blaez had expected Maelona to quickly dump the carcass off to the women who were tasked with preparing the meat and hides from the hunts, and then go directly to see the sorceress. Instead, she stayed with the women, looking over their tools and chatting with them, and then she began taking care of the carcass.

He wondered if he should ask her to go with him now, but he didn't want to increase this coolness that had been between them since the hunt. So Blaez headed off to see the sorceress on his own. After all, it was his duty to check in with the sorceress upon their return.

Unlike the other shifters in the village, Ailla Melyonen, or the sorceress as she was known to their people, did not live in a hut in the village. Rather, she lived in a cave whose entry-way was carved into the rocky side of an escarpment that jutted up from the forest on the northern edge of the village. This made sense, Blaez supposed, as it was more protected than the regular huts. He knew as well that she had mazes of tunnels and rooms upon rooms that continued deep under the escarpment, where she practiced her arts.

He knew this because he had been working as her assistant since he was a young boy, searching out items she required and helping her in any way she needed. In return, she helped him to battle his inner demons by pointing him in the direction of those who could use his help, and sometimes providing the means for him to help.

She had also been like a mother to him, taking him in and caring for him when he had no one else to do so. He owed her his life.

He entered this cave now and found Ailla sitting by the cozy fire in the reception room just past the entrance, preparing tea. She looked up expectantly and greeted him as if it were any other day and he had not just returned from a journey. She did not show any sign of surprise that he was alone.

"Sorceress Ailla," Blaez said while inclining his head to her in greeting.

"My dear Blaez, come and have some tea with me and tell me of your journeys. I take it things went smoothly?"

The sorceress had striking amethyst eyes and violet hair, and she looked not much older than Blaez himself. But she had a motherly way about her, and he knew she was much older than she looked. She had first taken him in as a boy, and they had been close ever since.

Blaez had grown and changed so much since his boyhood, yet the sorceress looked almost the same. Rumor said that sorcerers live an even longer lifespan than those of their own peoples, with the magic that flowed through them renewing their physical forms time and again. He was beginning to suspect this rumor was true.

"Yes, they did," Blaez responded, "though our guest does not seem inclined to come greet you at the moment. We hunted on the way in, and she stayed behind with the women to process the kill."

"I expected such," the sorceress replied. "She is going to need some time to adjust to the idea of being back here."

Blaez thought it interesting that Ailla had used 'back here.' So, Maelona had been here before, as Maelona herself had said, and the sorceress knew of her.

"I don't understand why you sent me to her, Sorceress, or why you didn't tell me more about her. She seems very capable of taking care of herself, and she seemed to know her way to our village quite well. I don't think you really sent me out there to guide and protect her. Do you not trust her?"

"I sent you, dear Blaez," the sorceress replied, "so you could get to know each other a little without pretense and prejudice before you realize who you are to each other. I also sent *you* specifically, my friend, because she could be the key to us surviving the dark times that are to come, but only if she heals old scars and becomes whole again. You and she can help each other there. You can help her heal. It is what you are destined to do.

"And besides," Ailla continued, "as strong and capable as she is, she is only one person. She cannot be everywhere at once, and she will need help if she is to succeed in her mission. She will need help if she is to survive." This last was spoken in a quiet, sad voice.

Blaez sat in silent thought for a moment. Then he asked, "Tell me, Sorceress, who is this woman, and why is she so important to our cause?"

Ailla turned to Blaez with a sad expression on her face. After a pause, she answered, "She is my daughter."

The words hit Blaez like a punch to the sternum. If Maelona Sima was the sorceress' only daughter, then he could only guess how she would respond once she discovered who he was. He didn't think it would be good.

"Wait," he said, "if she is your daughter I would have seen her around the village when I was a child. Why did I not recognize her?"

"Because, knowing her, she hasn't shown her true self to anyone since just before she left here more than forty years ago."

Chapter 4

The next morning, Blaez approached the hut where Maelona was staying. As she came into view, he paused to take in the sight of her sharpening her knives next to the hide of what he assumed was their stag. The hide was stretched out on a wooden frame.

Blaez had come to respect Maelona for her strength and self-sufficiency in the short time they had known each other. He believed they were beginning to understand one another; were becoming close. Now that he knew who she really was, however, he hesitated to approach her.

This is not the time to be a coward, he mentally chided himself, and then he set off toward her once again.

"Maelona Sima," he greeted as he approached.

Maelona looked at him with a small smile and a nod as she greeted him in return, "Blaez."

"The sorceress wishes to confer with us this morning."

As a reply, she wiped her knife on a soft piece of leather and stood. Then, returning the knife to its place on her hip, she turned to face him. "Let us be off then, shall we?"

Blaez breathed a small sigh of relief at Maelona's willingness to address the sorceress this morning. However, he sensed some lingering reluctance and a little sadness on her part as they walked to the sorceress' cave on the outskirts of the village. He could now guess at the reasons for that, as well as for her silence, as they walked along. He knew it had been some time since the sorceress had seen her daughter face to face. The sorceress had told him once that her daughter had left just a few months before he came into her care, a little over forty years ago. He now felt nervous that he was going to be witness to their reunion.

The sorceress stood waiting at the cave entrance as Maelona and Blaez approached. Blaez stayed back as Maelona approached her estranged mother. Maelona hesitated, but then the sorceress held her hands out toward her. "My darling Lona," she said, using her old pet name for her daughter, "it has been too long."

Maelona walked into her mother's arms. They stood each holding the other's forearms, forehead to forehead, nose to nose.

Maelona took a step back from her mother and looked up into her eyes. Her mother had hardly aged at all, and she had the same loving warmth in her smile and eyes. Maelona felt a sudden stab of guilt that she had left her mother alone for so long.

"I am so sorry that I have not come to see you in such a long time."

"I understand your reasons, my dear; do not fret. Still, I wish our reunion could have been during happier times."

"I have so much to apologize for, Mother, and there is much we need to discuss," Maelona said. She briefly glanced in Blaez's direction before looking back to her mother. "Perhaps we should speak alone for a time."

The sorceress looked to Blaez with a warm smile and reached out her hand to him. "My dear Lona, the three of us have much to discuss. We each have different parts of the same story to share with each other."

Maelona gazed at her mother questioningly, and her mother looked back at her with a small, sad smile. "Blaez," Ailla said, "is the son of Blyth Murdax."

Blaez watched as a myriad of emotions flitted across Maelona's usually calm exterior. From shock, disgust, panic, anger, and hatred, her face finally settled into a mask of sadness. She looked at her mother before looking back at Blaez. Then she turned and walked away.

In the few weeks he had known her, this was the first time Blaez had seen Maelona show so much clear emotion. After a silent moment or two, Ailla reached her hand out to Blaez once more and said, "Come, Blaez. We will have some tea. Then when we are done, you will go and speak with my Lona."

"Why would she ever want to speak to me again?" Blaez asked with a slow shake of his head.

"Because you are not your father, Blaez. Maelona knows that. Maybe some day you will come to accept it yourself."

An hour or so later, Maelona heard footsteps approaching from behind. She knew by the sound of the footfalls that it was Blaez. She was not surprised that he had found her. She had figured the sorceress would tell him where to look, and aside from that, she knew he had a sensitive enough sense of smell that he could track her scent easily. As he came close, she could hear that he was moving slowly, hesitantly, as if unsure whether to approach her.

Once he had gotten close, and the footsteps stopped, Maelona asked without turning around, "Do you know what this place is, Blaez?"

Maelona sat cross-legged at the edge of a large crater in the ground. It looked like a shallow bowl a couple of hundred meters across, with scorched earth spreading across it to the edges. The center held a circle of what looked like melted stone bleached white that was a couple of meters in diameter.

"My people call it the Crater of Sorrows," Blaez answered. "Though I was quite young when this came to be here, I have learned enough over the years to understand that this is the crater of *your* sorrows. I don't know all the details. My mother and the sorceress told me enough to know that this is the place where my 'father' and yours met their ends, and the place where evil tried to harm you. I have no other details. It is like the people think it bad luck to talk about it. I asked Ailla one time to tell me more about it, but she simply said it was your story to tell. At that time, I did not know that I would ever meet you."

After a short pause, Blaez continued, "I understand if you refuse to have me accompany you, but I really would like to help. I feel I *need* to help. It is my duty."

Maelona turned to look over her shoulder at Blaez, who stood a couple of feet behind her. She patted the ground beside her as she said, "Come sit with me, Blaez. Let me tell you the story."

Moving hesitantly at first, Blaez moved forward to sit beside her on the grass. Once he was settled, Maelona turned to look out over the crater again, and she began to speak.

"My mother, as you know, is a sorceress of the wolf shifters - your people. I do not know, however, if you are aware that my father was a sorcerer of the seer people. Each race of Sterrenvar has the potential to produce those capable of controlling the magic of the elements, but this is very rare. It usually only happens once every few generations.

"My father, being a seer, suspected dark times were coming…the dark times that are descending upon us now, in fact. He knew our realm could use all the help it could get, and he did not feel we had the luxury of waiting another generation or two to have more beings on the side of good that could control magic.

"As both a seer and a sorcerer, he had extra sensitivity to other magical beings. He knew of my mother, and he left his village to seek her out. So, you could say their pairing started as a partnership in securing our futures. But they came to love each other very much, and were very devoted to each other, even though they could not stay together all the time. My mother and her skills were needed here with the shifters, and my father was needed with his people. However, my father did come to visit us as often as his duties allowed.

"This creature you see here before you," she said, gesturing at herself, "is a product of both the shifter and the seer races, and the daughter of two magical beings. I am the result of their attempt to purposefully create another magical being. They were able to predict certain characteristics that I would have, but there were other things that they could not predict since I was the product of two different races. I am not the only one ever born in such a situation, and history has shown that the offspring of two different peoples can have any combination of traits from those peoples."

Maelona turned to look more fully at Blaez, shifting her body, so that she was almost facing him. "How much do you know about the seers, Blaez? I mean, aside from what I have told you on our journey here."

He thought for a moment before responding. "Well, I know that, like the shifter species, seers are extremely long-lived, in comparison to humans. Honestly, though, most of what I know about them is what you have told me…and that they tend to be secretive."

"It's true, seers are long-lived," Maelona replied. "In fact, they live longer than shifters. Where your people can live for seven hundred to eight hundred years, seers usually live for about one thousand years or more, barring illness or injury. Of course, you can consider the two life expectancies to be close in comparison to the humans' seventy or eighty years.

"Still, this difference in life expectancies left some questions as to how I would age and mature, such as when I would enter my adolescence, if I would be able to shift, if I would have magical abilities, and how powerful they would be. So, I lived my early years, up until I was 44 years old, sheltered in this village. I was watched carefully for clues as to how my development would progress, while remaining hidden and protected.

"Don't get me wrong," Maelona continued, "my parents loved me very much and ensured I had the proper education in all things both seer and shifter. They even made certain I learned basic survival and fighting skills. However, this was not enough to prepare me for the evils of the world."

"Evils such as my father," Blaez said in a somber tone. Maelona couldn't help but notice how the corners of his mouth turned down and his voice held a bit of a sneer as he said the word *father*.

Nodding and swallowing back a lump in her throat, Maelona continued. "Well, as it turns out, my adolescence did not begin at the age of twenty-five or thirty years, as what typically happens with shifters. We were not sure when it would happen, but as I passed my thirtieth year, it became a waiting game. It had been clear from an early age that I had some magical ability, but we would not know the extent until I passed that stage in my maturation.

"When I was forty-two, changes finally became apparent. My body started to develop into that of a young woman, and my magical abilities became stronger. I still had not shifted at that point, and we did not know if I would.

"My parents warned me that I would need to be careful with my use of magic and to keep my magical abilities private. Sorcerers are few and far between in our world, and many evil beings seek to either destroy us or enslave us to do their bidding.

"Since we tend to stand out because of our unusual hair and eye colors, many sorcerers prefer to stay hidden as much as possible. As my magic became more powerful, my father, during his visits to see my mother and I, started to instruct me in how to hide the traits that would make my identity apparent once I headed out into the world. He had me practice the seer skill of changing hair and eye color with him every time he came to visit. We seers are lucky that we have this ability to hide our features."

Blaez turned to study Maelona's profile, and her hair and eye color. Her mother's hair was violet and her eyes amethyst. The sorceress once explained to Blaez that, unlike most other creatures of Sterrenvar, sorcerers could have just about any coloring found in nature. Blaez found himself doubting now that the brown color of her eyes and hair were her true coloring, and he tried picturing her with her mother's hair and eye colors. That would most definitely cause her to stand out.

Blaez's attention was pulled back to Maelona's story as she continued: "Despite my father's training, I was young and naïve and thought myself safe here in the village. And for the most part, I was, with shifters generally having the propensity to do good. But there are always those few who choose to go against the inherent nature of their kind.

"I started noticing that your father often tended to be near where I was in the village, watching me. It wasn't long before

I realized he was following me. At first, I thought he was one of the people assigned by my mother to help protect me. She always had a couple of trusted protectors keeping an eye on me. Thankfully, it was usually from a distance, and never when I practiced magic. Then, one day in the market, I turned and saw Blyth looking at me with an expression I could only describe as…. covetous. It was unnerving."

Blaez perceived Maelona's slight shudder and had to suppress one of his own. The thought of his own father desiring a female as young as Maelona had been at the time…it disgusted him. He was ashamed to be related by blood to such a man.

He longed to say or do something to help comfort her right now. However, he did not know how such a self-sufficient creature would react to that, and he did not want to interrupt the story he had longed to know the details of for most of his life. So, he continued to sit quietly so she would continue.

"I used to practice my sorcery here in private. One day, while I was sitting in the middle of this clearing," she said while nodding toward the center of the crater, "practicing at changing the natural hues of the wildflowers around me, your father approached me from behind. I was concentrating so hard on what I was doing that I didn't notice his presence until he was upon me."

Blaez noted the haunted look on Maelona's face as she told the story, with raw emotions moving across her usually stoic features, and he knew she was reliving that day in her mind. He wished he could take those memories, that whole experience, from her. If he had known the truth of his father back then— aside from his cruelty at home—could he have done something to stop him?

"He said he knew someone who would give him a great reward for a 'creature' like me," Maelona continued, "but that he would be the first to possess me."

Maelona turned to look at Blaez. "I had begun physical training, but I had not yet taken it seriously. Also, I had only limited control over my magic." Her voice had begun to shake a little as she spoke. This was the first time Blaez had heard her speak with such emotion and unsteadiness in her voice, and he longed to be able to take her pain away. He suddenly felt afraid to hear the rest of her story.

But instead of continuing, Maelona slid down the side of the crater and began walking toward the center. Blaez followed.

"Your father grabbed me, hit me, and tossed me around. Initially, I was so shocked that I didn't even fight back. But when he started tearing at my clothes, it finally became clear to me what he intended to do. In that moment of intense fear and anger, I screamed, and there seemed to be an explosion of raw power and emotion torn from deep inside me. I saw nothing but a blinding white light, and then…nothing." Maelona paused for a few moments as she stared down at the bleached white stone in the middle of the crater.

Blaez's body shook with the force of the rage he felt toward his father in that moment. Maelona didn't need his anger, however. She needed his understanding. She needed someone to listen. So, he took a couple of deep, steadying breaths, trying to calm his emotions. When he felt more in control, he moved to face her so she would know that she had his full attention. Finally, she continued.

"When I awoke some time later, I was at my mother's sanctuary with her sitting beside me. She told me that my magic had responded to my extreme stress and agitation by creating a powerful, outward force like an explosion. Your father was killed instantly."

She nodded to a dark patch on the ground, and Blaez knew that was the spot where his father's life had ceased. He felt surprisingly little upon seeing this, aside from the residual anger that lingered after he had learned what his father had done, and had intended to do. Then Maelona walked toward the edge of the crater to the left of where they had been sitting, and he looked down to see that she was staring at another dark patch.

"Unfortunately, he was not the only casualty that day," Maelona said with a sad, quiet voice. "My father was a seer, as you know, and one night, not long before this incident, he had a vision of your father and his plans. My mother later told me that he had run into the village to find me. He told her that he had a dream-vision warning of your father's intentions. He could not see what happened to me, however, because of our limitations on seeing ourselves and those who directly affect our lives. He could only see your father and his plans for me. My father had been at the seer village, which is about a couple of weeks from here on foot, depending on how quickly you travel. Once he saw I was in danger, he ran straight here to try and save me."

Blaez looked up from the dark patch of ground at Maelona and noticed that her whole body had started to subtly shake. "I didn't even know he was here. He was trying to save me," she said in a quiet voice.

"As soon as I was strong enough and had perfected the ability to hide my features, I left for my father's village. It was my fault that they were now without their sorcerer, and I wanted to fill the hole I had caused. I also wanted to learn more about my father and his people."

Without thinking, Blaez moved forward to wrap his arms around her in comfort. "I am so sorry that happened to you, Maelona. You are not to blame. It was my own father's cruel actions that brought about this tragedy…all of it. I feel as though maybe I could have stopped it. My father was vicious to my mother and I as well. If only I had told a protector, maybe they could have stopped him before such a tragedy occurred.

"I want to assure you," he said forcefully as he continued to hold on to her, "that I am nothing like my father. I have fought all my life to never become like him, and to try to do what little I can to right some of the wrongs he committed. I wish I could go back in time so I could tell someone, anyone, what he was like so the protectors could have put a watch on him before any of this happened. I am so sorry I did not."

Blaez was startled momentarily when Maelona suddenly grabbed hold of his biceps and stepped back to look him in the eye.

"First," she said, "let me say this. The race we are born to, who our parents are, and even fate itself only partly determine who we become. More important than all these things are the choices we make and the intentions behind them. Regardless of the inherent natures of our races or our parentage, we get to choose who we want to be. In the end, it is our own choices and actions that truly make us who we are.

"I may not have known you long, Blaez," she added, "but I am a seer. We are very good at reading people and their intent. I can see your drive to do good, and not for a moment would I ever place you in the same category as your father. And even if I were inclined to do so, the fact that my mother thinks so highly of you speaks volumes. You cannot shoulder any of his blame. You were a young child at the time. These were his sins, not your own." With her gaze boring into his, she said earnestly, "I see who you are."

Blaez stared into Maelona's eyes, and he could see the sincerity burning there. Though he had been told practically the same thing numerous times in his life, he finally understood. Her opinion meant so much after what she had suffered at the hands of his kin. Finally, after all these years, he could feel some of the weight lifting from his shoulders.

Maelona stepped back and looked up at the sky. She took a deep breath before speaking again.

"In any case, Blaez," Maelona said, "I forgave your father years ago. It is myself I cannot forgive. I took the lives of two men, one of whom strived to be a good man, a kind man, every day of his life. The other will never have the opportunity to regret his mistakes and redeem himself for his actions." She looked back at Blaez and met his gaze, and she continued in a sad, regretful voice, "I may not have had full control of my magic, but I still ended two men's lives. They and their families, myself included, will never get back what was lost."

Looking down to the ground and speaking in a quiet, sad voice, she said, "I will work on my own redemption all the days of my life."

Maelona stared down into the crater for a few moments more. Then she said, "I have not used magic in the presence of others since that day, and I have avoided emotionally-charged situations for fear of losing control again. With these limitations, I could not completely fill my father's place in his village. To try and make up for this, I used the knowledge of herbs and healing plants my mother taught me to become a healer to the people. I also trained hard in many skills so I could be as useful to his people as possible without the use of magic."

Maelona hesitated, and it seemed as though she had something more to say. But instead of speaking she stood quietly, staring down at the black mark on the ground at her feet. After a few moments, she looked back up at Blaez. "Now let us go see the sorceress," she said. "We have much to prepare."

That same evening, Blaez, Maelona, and Ailla ate together at the sorceress' dwelling.

"Let Blaez and I fill you on some of what has happened here since you left." Ailla said. Then she nodded to Blaez.

"Not long after my father – well, not long after what happened," Blaez began, "my mother, Fionne Murdax, became very ill. An untreated wound, inflicted by my father not long before he passed, had become badly infected. It had been festering for some time, but she refused to seek help. She also forbade me to do so on her behalf. I was young and had always been respectful of my mother's wishes. I was also very protective of my mother, especially after witnessing what she had endured for so long. For a long time, I warred with myself, torn between doing as she instructed, or protecting her from harm."

Blaez paused and took a deep breath before continuing. "When it became clear, even to my inexperienced child's mind, that my mother would not to be able to heal on her own this time, I went to your mother for help. But I had waited too long." He leaned forward toward the fire, forearms on his lap, and hung his head. "It was too late.

"When my mother passed, I had no one. There was no one willing to help the orphaned son of the evil Blyth Murdax. No one except your mother," Blaez said to Maelona while nodding toward the sorceress. "Even though it was my own father that had harmed her daughter, she took me in and ensured I was educated and trained as a protector, as all the village youth are. She also taught me about plants and herbs, including what can hurt and what can heal. She eventually employed me as her assistant, hunting out ingredients she may need."

"And a very good assistant he has proven himself to be," the sorceress said with a smile.

Smiling back at her, Blaez continued, "Ailla understood my drive to prove to myself and others that I am more than my father's son. I yearned to ease some of the suffering and damage he left in his wake. So, when someone needed aid that I could give, she pointed me in their direction."

Blaez looked up at Maelona and said, "She became like a mother to me." He hoped this admission would not cause her pain, given the distance between Maelona and her mother throughout these past forty years.

As if she could read his mind, Maelona gave a small smile and responded in a soft voice, "I am glad you were there for each other, and happy she had you to keep her company and keep her safe when I could not."

Ailla stirred in her seat, looking like she wanted to say something but not knowing if she should. Finally, she decided to speak.

"Lona, my love, we understand...*I* understand, why you went away. No one here will judge you. Everyone has to deal with life's trials in their own way, and that was yours. It was even noble in many ways, wanting to make up your father's loss to those in his village who needed him.

"However, as a sorceress, and as your mother, I am very concerned about your refusal to use your magic. It is a part of you, my dear, and denying it is denying yourself. I want you to have as many advantages as you can, knowing what likely lies ahead for you."

"What does lie ahead, exactly?" Blaez asked. "Maelona has spoken to me about the danger involved in her mission. She warned me I might not want to help once I knew what it was. Now, Ailla, you speak of wanting Maelona to have all the advantages she can. What is it we're facing?"

"War, my dear Blaez," Ailla answered. "War against a very formidable opponent and his many, formidable allies. It is a long and complicated story, my friend, and you will hear all the details soon enough."

After a brief pause, Maelona spoke again. "Don't worry, Mother," she said. "I have said I do not practice in the presence of others, but that does not mean I do not practice my magical skills at all. My goal is to not lose control of my magic. At some point, I realized that by trying to constantly suppress it I was not controlling my power. Instead, I was allowing it to control me.

"I have many free evenings when you shifters need to sleep, and the seer in me does not," she said. "I spend my time preparing, gathering, or making what we need, practicing my martial arts and weapons skills, and attempting my magic."

"I am so glad to hear that, my daughter. It will give me comfort during your upcoming trials and battles to know that you are well-prepared. Perhaps you and I could practice together some evenings. I'm sure I could go without sleep for a night here and there to have the privilege of working with you, doing all I can to ensure your safety."

"I would like that, Mother," Maelona replied with a warm smile. "I would like that very much."

Chapter 5

A few days later, the gray pre-dawn light was upon the village when Maelona burst into Blaez's hut, jolting him awake.

"Blaez," she called as she entered. "Wake up! We need to go – now!"

Blaez didn't know what was going on, but hearing the urgency in Maelona's voice, he jumped up and took off after her. Just outside the village, he shifted into wolf form so he could more easily keep up with her pace while using his heightened senses to alert him of danger.

They ran without slowing for what felt to Blaez like a couple of hours. Finally, Maelona stopped running and crouched low to the ground. Blaez followed suit.

"Listen," Maelona said. After staying still and listening intently for a moment, Blaez heard what seemed to be the sounds of fighting and swords clashing. Keeping low, Maelona made her way forward until she could look out into the clearing ahead. She was careful to stay hidden.

In the middle of the clearing, three creatures were attacking what appeared to be a human male. These creatures were taller and broader than any human male, and each of them had skin that varied in color from light gray to almost black. Their faces looked like distorted versions of human faces, like they had swollen and had been pulled out to the sides.

"Demonkin," Maelona whispered.

The human male fought valiantly with sword and fist, but

he was outnumbered, and it was apparent that he was losing the battle. Maelona leaned close to Blaez so she could speak quietly to him. "Stay in your wolf form until I tell you it's safe to change back. Circle around to the other side of the clearing and wait for my signal to attack."

Blaez did as instructed, and he made his way around, all the while keeping an eye on the battle in front of him. A moment after he had reached the other side, he heard a wordless battle cry. He looked up to see Maelona jumping from an overhanging tree branch, wielding a short sword, onto the back of the demonkin nearest to her. Blaez then jumped into action by attacking the demonkin closest to him.

Blaez tore into his opponent with claw and fang, all the while dodging strikes from the demonkin's dull blade. As soon as he saw an opening, he lunged for the demonkin's throat, crushing his windpipe as he twisted his body and threw the demonkin to the ground. When he was certain the demonkin would not get up again, he looked up to find Maelona.

The first demonkin that Maelona had attacked lay lifeless in a heap a few feet behind her. The human was on the ground, trying and failing to get up. He was obviously injured. Maelona had now become engaged in a fight with the demonkin who had attacked the human. Blaez felt the urge to attack the demonkin and protect Maelona, but he hesitated as he took in the sight before him.

Maelona danced around the large demonkin, striking out with feet and hands whenever an opening presented itself. Though she wielded her sword, she did not rely solely on the weapon as many would have done. Instead, she used her whole body as a weapon and the sword as just an extension and a defense.

Though large and strong, the demonkin was overcome by Maelona's agility and skill within moments. As the demonkin swung its sword in an arc toward Maelona, she moved toward its body and thrust her sword into its chest. It became clear that she had hit her intended target when the demonkin shuddered and then dropped to the ground. Maelona quickly hopped out of the way.

Maelona turned and went to the downed human, kneeling next to him. Blaez padded over to her side, still in wolf form, and looked down upon the human male. He was bloodied, battered, and barely conscious. Maelona looked at the man's face, then she looked down to where an amulet hung by a chain from his neck.

"Where did you get this?" Maelona asked the man.

She looked up once again as the man ground out in a hoarse voice, "Maddock," before succumbing to unconsciousness.

Maelona quickly undid a clasp at her side and swung her pack from her back to her front. "You will need your hands, Blaez," Maelona said, and he quickly shifted back to human form. She pulled out some leaves and some bandages and handed them to Blaez.

"Press the leaves against his wound here," she instructed Blaez while pointing out a large wound in the man's chest. "Then bandage it up. Cover him to keep him warm." She pulled a thin cloak out of her pack and handed it to him. "We need to get him back to my mother as quickly as possible."

Maelona took off into the woods while Blaez tended to the stranger's wounds. Thanks to the Sorceress, he recognized the leaves Maelona gave him as leighis leaves, which had great healing properties. This human was very lucky that Maelona had happened to have some in her pack.

A short time later, Maelona returned with a sleigh such as the one she had made to pull the deer carcass. She laid it down next to the man and then moved to his other side to check him out for other injuries.

"He also has a broken leg, so be careful when we move him," Maelona said. Blaez helped her move the man onto the sleigh, as gently as possible, and they began to pull it back in the direction they had come. They moved as quickly as they could without jostling him too much.

"Why were there demonkin here, so close to the village?" Blaez questioned as they traveled. "Inside the Foraoise Naofa? Evil has never ventured inside the Sacred Forest before."

"It has," Maelona replied. "But not in millennia."

"What about the magical defenses the Sorcerers of the Light placed on the forest?" Blaez asked. "How could these demonkin just walk right in here? What do you think this means?"

"I think it means: take a good look around you and take it all in, my friend," Maelona replied. "Enjoy the beauty of nature all around us in our forest. Breathe it all in. Spend time with your friends. Cherish them. But do it all in between training sessions. Because if we are not victorious in the war to come, none of this will be the same again.

"If the dark sorcerer has this much magical influence now, if he could breach defenses put in place by a group of the realm's most powerful sorcerers, then if he is successful with his plans he could tear us all apart."

They walked on in silence for a while before Blaez asked, "Do you think it's possible, Maelona? Do you think we will be able to defeat them?"

"I don't know, Blaez. Already, I feel violated that they were able to breach our precious forest. They have surely already breached some human settlements by now. Already, many likely feel as we do right now, or worse. So, the one thing I do know for certain is this: I will do whatever I have in my power to do, to save our beautiful realm from the darkness. It may be flawed, but it is ours. All of ours. And we must protect it."

Blaez eyed the unconscious man with suspicion. "We don't know this man," Blaez said to Maelona. "How do we know it's safe to bring him to the village? There are women and children there. We like to keep our home hidden from outsiders, especially now, with the threat of war on the horizon."

"The amulet," Maelona replied, glancing back to the unconscious form on the sleigh behind them. "He wears an amulet that is only gifted by the seer elders to trusted friends and allies of the seer people. It grants safe passage through seer territories, and aid in times of need. I think I know who he is, thanks to the amulet and my vision, but I don't yet know his character. He also looks like someone I once knew well. If I am right, and his father is who I think he is, then he was sent to us for a reason.

"In any case, we will bring him to the Sorceress' sanctuary

and keep him away from the village. When we leave again, we will take the north path so we will not have to pass close to your people. He is human, and he is too young to have received the amulet directly from my father. We will stay cautious and vigilant until we know more about him."

"Your father?" Blaez questioned.

"Yes. The name he gave…it was my father's name," Maelona replied.

Looking down at the injured man, Blaez commented, "He would never make it as far as the seer village. It seems we have no choice." Then, after a moment of thought, he asked, "should we send someone to your village to alert them when we arrive?" he asked.

"There is no point," Maelona replied. "If the amulet was indeed given by my father, it falls to me now to honor its promise."

Blaez could hear the sadness in her voice when she spoke of her father. He had the urge to put an arm around her in comfort, but with each of them holding one side of the sleigh, it was an impossible feat.

They continued the rest of the journey to the shifter village in silence, conserving their breath and their strength for transporting the stranger to the help he so desperately needed.

When they were about a half an hour out from the village, Maelona and Blaez came upon a wolf protector on sentry duty doing his rounds.

"I am glad to see you, Caellum," Blaez greeted, not needing the warrior to shift to know who he was. "We have an injured man here. He will need the skills of the sorceress. Please, run ahead and let her know of our arrival."

The wolf nodded his head in acknowledgment and took off toward the village.

When they reached the village, a crowd of townsfolk in both human and wolf form had gathered. The sorceress came forward to greet them and to take a look at their guest. "Come, quickly," she said. "Bring him to my sanctuary."

Once they arrived at the sorceress' dwelling, they moved the injured man into one of the many rooms carved into the rock that made up her sanctuary. Ailla had a cot ready, a fire burning, and a pot steaming above the fire. There were also several vessels containing various items laid out on a table by the bedside.

As soon as the man had been placed upon the cot, the sorceress got to work removing his clothing and checking his injuries. "Leighis leaf," she said as she came upon the dressing Maelona had Blaez place on his chest wound. "Good. How soon after his injuries was this placed on the wound?"

"Within a few minutes," Blaez replied. "Maelona carried some in her pack. It saved us much time, as I would have had to search for it." Looking over to Maelona with a small smile, he commented, "It's hard to carry weapons and supplies when you have to shift back and forth from one form to another."

The sorceress began her treatment of the injured man by exposing and cleaning his wounds. She talked and explained as she worked, having become accustomed to training first her daughter, and then her apprentice.

"I am making a compress from the leighis leaf, boiled in water with some added herbs to help numb the pain. Once it has thickened enough, we will place it on his wounds to help them heal more quickly.

"When he has regained consciousness and can take fluid, we will give him a tea made with plants and herbs that will help with reducing pain, fever, and swelling." Once she got to his leg, she looked up at Blaez and said, "Unfortunately, if we were to treat his broken leg without the use of magic, healing it would take more time than you have to spare. So, once he can take a remedy for pain, I will realign the fracture and fuse it using my magic. It will take some time to heal fully, but it will take a fraction of the time to heal than it would take using only traditional methods."

Blaez knew from working with the sorceress for years that she, like all sorcerers, channeled magic from the energies found in nature and the elements around them. They drew it into themselves and then focused it to do their bidding. It took many years of practice to be able to always focus this magic when and where you needed it, and even more years to learn to do it quickly and efficiently. Even then, this process consumed a lot of energy. After many centuries of practice, the more powerful feats of magic, like healing serious injuries, still left the sorceress exhausted and physically drained.

"Don't push yourself too much, Sorceress. Take care of yourself as well."

"Don't worry, Blaez," she replied. "I'm old enough to know my limitations."

Blaez found himself now wondering about Maelona's magic. From what she had told him, she had pretty much turned her back on her magic. He felt guilty for the years of practice lost to Maelona due to his own father's evil actions and disappointed that she would not have this added strength to rely upon to protect her in the battles that would surely come. It was up to him then, he decided, to give her back some of that strength and protection she had lost by always having her back.

Chapter 6

Gareth came awake slowly, first registering the smell of herbs, and then the sound of a fire crackling. Though he felt the warmth of the fire, he quickly became aware of some other, less pleasant sensations as well, such as the searing pain in his chest and many sore muscles. His eyes flickered open, and he stared up at a ceiling of solid, dark gray rock. He turned his head to the left and saw more rock. He decided he must be in a cave of some sort.

He then turned his head to the right and jumped with a start when he found a person sitting next to him, rather close, looking at him intently.

"By Father's beard!" He cursed as his startled jump caused excruciating pain to shoot through his leg.

Once the pain had subsided a little and he had calmed down, he looked up again to find the person still staring at him with the same stoic expression as before, studying his features. The corner of his mouth began to rise in a smug smirk when he realized the person was female... a rather attractive female at that, with long, shiny chestnut hair and deep brown eyes. His smug smirk fell quickly, however, once she began to speak.

"You are the Prince of Eastgate, are you not?" she asked. Her expression was serious and her eyes inquisitive.

"Yes," he replied hesitantly, a little surprised by the sudden, blunt question coming from a complete stranger. "Yes," he said again, more strongly this time. "I am Gareth, son of Niall, King of Eastgate." Maelona nodded slightly at his response.

"Well, Gareth, son of Niall, I am Maelona, daughter of Maddock." Then she placed a cup in his hand and said, "Here, drink this. It will help with the pain."

As the mention of Maddock's name sunk in, he began to remember his mission, his days of walking in the woods alone, and his attack by demonkin. And then he remembered someone leaping from the trees to come to his aid.

"It was you, wasn't it? You jumped into the fight to help me."

"Unfortunately, not soon enough it would seem. The demonkin managed to stab you in the chest before I could get to you. You were very lucky that no vital organs were hit."

"Still, I have the feeling I wouldn't be alive now if it weren't for you."

"I can't take all the credit," Maelona replied. "I had some help," she said, nodding toward the corner.

Gareth followed her gaze to the corner and jumped again when he saw a huge black wolf. It had striking blue eyes that stood out in bright contrast against the dark color of its fur. Then he cursed again and said, "I have to stop doing that. My leg hurts like hell every time I move. Sorry, you'll have to forgive the language."

"Drink the tea," Maelona reminded him. "It will help ease the pain."

Gareth looked warily over at the large black wolf again as he sipped his tea.

"This is Wolf. He took down one of the demonkin that attacked you and helped me bring you here."

Gareth looked from the wolf back to Maelona, thinking that it was strange that she would introduce him to her wolf. But then again, many people were strange when it came to their animal companions.

"You named your wolf, Wolf?" he questioned with a grin. Maelona simply shrugged a shoulder.

"Well, I am grateful for his help, and for yours." Though he still felt weak, he managed to flash her a smile that had won over numerous others in the past - but she remained stoic and impassive.

After a moment, she replied, "The sorceress will be here shortly to tend to your leg." Then she turned and began walking out of the room, the large wolf following in her wake.

"Wait," Gareth called out to her. "You said you were the daughter of Maddock? Where is he? I need to speak to him immediately on a matter of some urgency."

Maelona paused in her step but did not turn around. "My father passed back into the universe many years ago," she replied. "You will speak with me...once you have healed a little." With that, she continued to stride out of the room.

Soon after Gareth awoke the next morning, Maelona and the Sorceress entered and came over to sit at his bedside.

"How are you feeling this morning, Gareth?" Ailla asked her patient.

"I am feeling much better, thank you, Sorceress." Gareth replied. "There is hardly any pain anymore. Thank you for your care during the night. You must not have gotten much rest yourself."

"Do not worry about me. I did not lose any sleep. My kind does not need as much sleep as yours does."

Gareth wondered if she meant 'her kind' as in sorcerers, or if there were something more to the comment.

"We had hoped to give you a little more time to heal before speaking with you, but we received some information during the night that leads us to believe we may not have much time," Ailla said, glancing at Maelona.

Gareth attempted to sit up more in the bed, but he winced in pain as he did so. Ailla grabbed a couple of pillows and propped them behind his back.

"Why don't we start with you telling us why you are here," Maelona said.

"My father knew your father years ago," Gareth began.

"Yes. I knew your father as well," Maelona replied.

Gareth gazed at her with a puzzled look. He knew his father was just a boy when he met Maddock. His father had told him he traveled into the Sacred Forest with his father, Gareth's grand-father. He had never gone back to that village since, as far as Gareth knew. So, it confused him how this girl, who looked younger than he did himself, could have known his father. She looked as if she may be in her early twenties compared to his twenty-six years.

Then again, his father did travel in secret from time to time, so he supposed it may have been possible that he traveled back here. His head was still groggy with sleep, and the tea he'd been taking for the pain didn't help. His head hurt when he tried to think through the fog, so he let it go and continued with his account.

"I don't know how much you know about Eastgate, but legend passed down from generation to generation says that the town is built upon something powerful, something that we are tasked to protect. The exact nature of what that is has been kept secret, passed down from king to king. Each king would tell their oldest sons all the details they were missing once they thought they were ready."

Gareth huffed out a short, humorless laugh before adding, "He doesn't think I'm ready yet, even though he does, obviously, think I'm ready to send to the sacred forest on this search for Maddock Sima. He didn't provide me with a map or any other details; he simply told me what direction to walk in and said Maddock or his people would find me.

"Turns out he was right," he said, smiling at Maelona. "Too bad it wasn't just a little sooner," he continued as he rubbed his hand over his bandaged chest with a wince.

"Back to why I am here," he went on. "For the past couple of months, our outer defenses have been under attack. There seems to be no rhyme or reason to the timing of the attacks, or to the areas being attacked. My father believes they are testing us, looking for weaknesses in our defenses. Then, three weeks ago, a guard turned up dead inside the castle walls. It seems almost inconceivable that such a thing could happen. My father's theory is that somehow our enemies got close enough to one of our trusted inner circle to sway them to their cause.

"At this point my father decided to send me to Maddock, to ask for help ferreting out the traitor. He says that what we are protecting is too important to leave to chance."

Gareth took a deep breath, shifting his gaze down toward the floor before continuing. "A couple of days before I left, my father started to feel under the weather. It's not like him. He never gets sick. Yet he was pale, weak, and sweating enough that my sister and I noticed. He tried to play it off as nothing serious, but I must say that I worried that maybe whoever killed that guard had gotten too close to my father as well. I tried to convince him to let me put off this journey so I could look out for him, but he said that he was fine; my sister could look after him. And if someone were getting that close to him, then my journey was now more important than ever."

The others had been silent as he told his tale. He looked up to see the sorceress leaning toward him, clearly interested in his story; Maelona sitting back looking at him with a curious expression on her face; and the wolf staring intently at him from the corner, as always. The wolf's stare gave him the shivers.

Finally, he looked back to Maelona and said, "My father, the king, was convinced that Maddock would help, but now I find that he is no longer here to help. Do you know anyone who can help us now?"

"Yes. I will help you," Maelona replied solemnly.

Maelona warred a little with herself, trying to decide how much to tell Gareth. After a moment, she leaned forward in her seat toward him and began to speak.

"You said your father does not think you ready yet to tell you the truth," Maelona began, "yet he sent you to my father, to our village, knowing you would learn the truth. He did believe you are ready."

Maelona watched Gareth's facial reactions as she spoke. His expression indicated that knowing that his father finally thought he was ready touched him, though he tried hard to hide his emotions.

"Did he tell you anything at all about my father, other than his name and that you could find him in the forest?" She asked.

"Just that he is a good man who can be trusted, and that he helps to protect the same thing that we protect."

"My father was a seer." Maelona announced. "I am a seer."

Maelona watched as Gareth's eyes grew wide and his expression distrustful.

"Do you think your father is a good man, Gareth?" She asked quietly.

"The best," Gareth replied.

"Do you trust him?"

"Of course," he said. "I would trust him with my life."

"And your father trusted us," Maelona said. "So, throw away the things you think you know, the things you learned from rumors and whispered stories. Believe in your father now, and open your mind to learn about us yourself."

"Did you just read my mind?" Gareth asked warily.

Maelona shook her head. "Of course not. We don't read minds. We can do many things, but we cannot do that."

"Then how…"

"What you were thinking was written all over your face," she explained.

"One thing we can do is see," Maelona continued. "Though our abilities in that area have also been greatly exaggerated.

"Last night I had a dream-vision. In it, I saw who was behind the targeted attacks on Eastgate. Well, not actually who was behind it. More like who is doing the attacking."

"Who?" Gareth asked eagerly.

"Demonkin."

"Demonkin?" Gareth exclaimed while trying to get up. He winced in pain, and Ailla stood to place a hand on his chest and push him back into a semi-reclining position.

"That's not all," Maelona said. "There will be a full-scale attack on Eastgate soon."

"What? Could you tell when?" Gareth asked.

"I could tell enough to know that we have time, but we still need to get you healed as soon as possible. That means you need to rest and do everything the sorceress tells you."

"I know you'll want to get back as soon as you can," the sorceress said. "However, you must wait a few days before you can go anywhere, Gareth. My magic can heal you much faster than you would heal on your own, but it will still take a little time. Your chest wound is almost fully healed; you are very lucky that nothing vital was hit. Your leg, however – it was a compound fracture, broken in a number of places, and with bone protruding through your shin." Gareth made a face at this information.

"I must use my magic on it for a short time," Ailla explained, "and then wait a while before I can do it again. If I rush it, it may not heal correctly. It should not take more than a few days, assuming you cooperate and do as I tell you between treatments."

"Sorceress," Maelona said, "I am calling a meeting for tonight, after the evening meal. We will meet with a group of the local tribe's warriors so we can start preparing for what is to come. You are welcome to come and observe or offer advice, if you like."

Ailla turned to look at Maelona inquisitively. Maelona simply nodded in response to her unspoken question, and then she said, "I will take my leave." With a nod to Gareth and the sorceress, she headed to the door, calling to the wolf to follow her on her way.

PART II:
THE JOURNEY

The journey of life takes twists and turns,
It follows no straight line.
It may veer away from what was planned
To follow your heart and mind.
The bravest of those among us follow
The paths we do not know,
And we grow the most as people when
We let our worst fears show.
When things look their darkest, we must keep
Moving to the light.
We must push aside the fears and doubts
And keep our goals in sight.

Chapter 7

Once outside the sorceress' cave, Blaez shifted back to human form. He grabbed a pair of light pants he kept hidden in a hollowed-out alcove near the sanctuary's entrance and dressed quickly. Wolf shifters were not usually shy about their natural forms, but he felt that making an attempt to always be clothed in the sorceress' presence was a sign of respect to her and her station. She was almost always in her human form as it was easier to control elemental magic. So, he always left some clothing near the entrance, just in case.

Once dressed, he turned to Maelona and asked, "What do you think about Gareth's story? Is he telling the truth? Do you think we can trust him?"

"I did not sense any deception from him," Maelona responded, "but I did learn some things from observing him. He cares deeply for his father. His concern for him is real. I also believe that his father was correct about him not being quite ready for the responsibilities of being King of Eastgate. He has the demeanor of a boy who has not yet seen the darker side of life, who has not known real sorrow or hardship. He is loyal and trustworthy, but his inexperience could make it easy for him to be manipulated. I don't think we should tell him everything there is to know about us quite yet, such as the nature of our peoples, though there may come a time when we can, or must."

"Regardless of whether or not we think him quite ready, I do not think we can afford the luxury of waiting long to explain the situation to him. Apparently, King Niall did not think so either. Gareth will need time to fully realize the extent of what is at stake, and he will need to prepare himself both mentally and physically. I won't know until I see Niall the exact nature or seriousness of his illness, and I certainly hope my old friend is not at death's door. However, Gareth needs to be prepared, just in case. Eastgate cannot be left unprotected.

"Also," Maelona said, "I can't be sure, but his body language when speaking of his sister, and to myself and the sorceress, lead me to believe he holds a limited view on the abilities of women. However, it could also be that he feels the need to protect them." Then, as she stared ahead with a smirk on her face and a glint in her eye, she continued, "His sister is going to turn his beliefs on their head."

Since the earlier conversation suggested she would not have ever met the king's daughter, Blaez figured this meant she had experienced a vision of the girl. *Strange how her knowing things others do not seems almost normal to me now*, Blaez mused.

"Was there anything else you saw in your visions?" Blaez asked.

Maelona looked at him as if she were trying to decide whether or not to share what was on her mind. Then she said, "Walk with me to the village, and I will tell you on the way."

They headed out, and Maelona began to speak. "The battle at Eastgate will only be the beginning," she said. "However, up to this point, neither I nor the other seers have been able to get a clear picture of the person leading these demonkin. In fact, we didn't foresee demonkin in the forest either. I am worried about what that means for the humans between here and the northern mountains. The attacks on the humans may have advanced further than what we expected them to by this point."

"Is it unusual for you to not be able to see things clearly?" Blaez asked.

"We don't pick and choose what we see. We are sent visions of where we are needed," Maelona reminded him. "In this case though, it is more like we are being sent visions, but someone or something is interfering with us seeing them clearly."

Blaez may just be learning about the seers and their abilities, but it certainly did not seem like a good thing if someone was able to block the vision of a race that was rumored to be one of the most powerful in the realm.

"There is also something else I have been getting in my visions that has been bothering me, but I don't know where it fits," Maelona said.

"What is it?" he asked.

"I've been getting flashes of a child – a boy. So far, I have not gotten more than the impression of his emotions. He is filled with anger, pain, and desire for revenge."

"What do you think it means?"

"I can't be certain at this point, but I think I might be seeing this dark sorcerer as a child. He has been blocking us from seeing parts of his present, but now it seems like his past may be sneaking through."

"Well, that's good, right?" Blaez asked. "If you can't see what he's doing now, maybe seeing into his past might give you an idea of his motivations and his plans."

"Yes, but so far, I haven't been given a lot to go on. I hope future visions will give us more."

Turning his thoughts back to the task at hand, he looked over to Maelona and asked, "So what now? What are our next steps?"

"Well, firstly," Maelona replied, "we need to invite as many protectors as are available to the meeting tonight. We must schedule practices to hone the skills we will need during the dark times to come. I believe the best place for us to start is with physical combat. When we meet tonight, we will ask the protectors to join us for practice beginning tomorrow. You and I will be partners-in-arms, so we should be familiar with each other's fighting style. I hope that we will even eventually learn to complement each other, fighting in tandem. We can practice with each other first to become comfortable with each others' fighting style before we begin training and practicing with the others."

Given what Blaez had learned of Maelona thus far, he found himself feeling excited about training with her. Maybe he could learn some things from her, and maybe, just maybe, he would be able to teach her a few things as well. He felt the smile grow on his face as he asked, "When do we begin?"

Maelona returned his smile and responded, "Let's go to the village to find some lunch first. We can begin once we have added some fuel to our fires."

Half an hour later, Maelona was sitting at a wooden table off to the side of a large open area in the town's center. Most of the pack came and went here at meal times, as it was customary to eat together whenever duties allowed. Maelona watched on as Blaez took advantage of this opportunity to spread word of the meeting to any protectors who were present, trusting them to spread the word along as well.

Maelona chewed an apple from one of the many trees off the southwest side of the village as she watched Blaez interact with some of the pups from the pack. He was play-fighting with them, but Maelona recognized the bigger benefit to this type of play. Shifter young did not start shifting until puberty, so this game also taught them some basic hand-to-hand techniques that could come in handy if danger came their way.

Maelona found herself a little in awe of Blaez as she thought of all the inconspicuous things Blaez did for others time and again, from playing with and teaching the young ones, to taking part in protector duties. And, of course, he had also helped her own mother for the last forty years, when she had not been in the correct frame of mind to do so herself. For that, she would be forever grateful.

Turning from Blaez, Maelona looked around at all the energetic and joyful signs of life to be found here, in the heart of the village. Not far from the group of young ones play fighting with Blaez, another group of youth played hunters and prey. Closer to the center of the common area, there were numerous booths set up where people could trade various items and get food. Groups of young and old alike sat eating their midday meal together, talking animatedly. Some sat at tables and others sat in the grass.

At one table, a group of young had various containers of inks and different sized needles strewn around them. They were practicing inking their marks onto pieces of animal hide. Wolf shifter young learned how to ink their marks before they learned how to write their names. Each young would create his or her own mark, practicing it until it was just the way they wanted. They then used this mark throughout their lives to represent themselves. It was their signature and their symbol.

Maelona's mind went back to when she first created and practiced her own mark along with other young her age, many years ago. She was light and carefree back then, when her only worry was getting that mark to be just the perfect representation of herself and still have time afterward to play with her few friends. For the first time since she left the shifter village, Maelona allowed herself a moment to feel nostalgic for what she had left behind.

Just as when she had left the seer village and looked back down upon it, reality now struck her again as she looked at all this life surrounding her; the laughter, the joy, the freedom, the love. This was what she, and many others like her would soon be fighting to protect. This was what was at stake.

She sat here in the village center today, feeling the freedom, energy, and goodness all around her, and it made her feel that much more determined to stand up against any evil that threatened to destroy it.

Her imagination went to a place where these young were pried from their families at a young age, forced to serve masters who thought themselves better and more powerful than them. She imagined them mistreated and beaten, fed only what was necessary for them to remain strong enough to serve their *masters*. She imagined them trading in play time for the many menial tasks involved in pampering creatures who are actually capable of taking care of themselves. And she suddenly found her rage reaching a boiling point.

Just then, Blaez finished his game with the young shifters and made his way back to Maelona, interrupting her silent raging. "Shall we?" he asked. She took a moment to breathe deeply and relax. Then she nodded to him, and they headed out to practice.

It did not take long for Blaez and Maelona to reach the clearing on the outskirts of the village where the protectors came regularly to hone their skills. As they entered the clearing, Maelona said, "Let's begin with hand-to-hand skills. We can work our way up to various weapons."

"I am a shifter," Blaez replied. "I have built in weapons. This would not be fair to you."

Maelona laughed a big, warm laugh, and Blaez could not help but grin along with her. Such a laugh was a rare gift from Maelona, and he had never seen her laugh with anyone but himself.

"I assure you, Blaez, that even in your wolf form, a hand to hand fight with me would still be fair. I do not sleep as often as you do, so I have much time during the night to devote to other pursuits, such as physical training. Also, I've been taught by the best martial trainer in the realm.

"When I first went to the seer village," she explained, "the elders knew I would be in much danger in the future because of who I am. Refusing to use my magic left me at a further disadvantage. So, the elders ensured I underwent stringent physical, martial arts, and weapons training so that I would be capable of protecting myself. They assigned their best fighter to teach me."

Then she turned to look fully at Blaez. "And therefore, we are starting here, Blaez. Some of the first, yet essential, lessons Donogh taught me are: know your enemy, yet never take anything for granted; never assume you are better than your opponent; be prepared for the unexpected, and *be* unexpected. Also, train your weaknesses, so they become strengths.

"Any opponent who knows you are a shifter might assume you will depend on the strength, speed, teeth, and claws of your wolf. You need to make sure you are equally formidable in your human form to prepare for this and other eventualities. Shifters are more dextrous in human form. Maybe you will be attacked while completing a task you need your human hands for. Maybe a sorcerer will lock you into your human form..."

"Is that possible?" Blaez interrupted, his voice laced with shock and concern.

Maelona glanced at Blaez and replied in a softer tone, "It is not common, to be sure, but it has happened." She looked at Blaez thoughtfully for a moment. Then she said, "I wish to demonstrate for you some of a wolf's vulnerabilities. I want you to shift into your wolf form and attack me. I will defend first with a weapon, and then without."

Maelona walked a dozen or so feet away from Blaez and turned to face him. As usual, she wore her typical leather outfit with straps crisscrossing her body and weapons in various holsters in the straps. Now she reached up behind to her lower back. When she brought her hand back around, she held what looked to be a cylinder about a foot long. Holding it in front of her in one hand, palm down, she clicked a button and the cylinder extended into a short staff about four feet long.

"Shift," she said.

Blaez turned his back, removed his pants and shifted into his beautiful, black wolf.

"Attack me."

Blaez paused for just a moment before running toward her. As he moved, Maelona crouched down, switching her grip to the ends of the short staff. Just as Blaez jumped up to lunge at her, Maelona jumped as well, straight at him, with the staff held horizontally in front of her. She rammed the staff into his open mouth, driving it back as far as it would go, essentially locking his jaw open. If the staff had been wooden, he could have snapped it easily. But Blaez could taste that it was some kind of metal...*strong* metal. If he were a real animal instead of a shifter, he was sure he would have lost some teeth.

He had barely a moment to think about this before he realized Maelona had flipped herself up and over the staff, and his head, twisting around to face front as she did so. She now sat astride Blaez's back. She held the staff firmly as she jerked her body to the side, using her body weight to throw him off balance.

As Blaez fell sideways to the ground, Maelona leaped off his back again while keeping the pressure on the staff. When they came to a stop, Blaez lay on his back on the ground, looking up at the inverted face of Maelona who knelt on one knee, bending over him and pressing down on the staff. Blaez tried to twist to the side to right himself, but Maelona did not budge, and he could not find any purchase. He felt like a turtle, upside down on his shell. He was also drooling considerably. The staff pressing back in his mouth kept it open and made it almost impossible for him to move his tongue.

"From here, I could perform several different killing blows," Maelona spoke seriously, looking down into Blaez's eyes. Then she got up and stood in front of him as he righted himself.

"That," she continued, "didn't even use all of my strength. Locking the jaws on an animal shifter has somewhat the same effect as a joint lock on people. If it is done effectively, you can control your enemy and gain the upper hand with relatively little effort.

"Again," Maelona commanded. "This time I will use no weapons." With that she stalked off away from him, retracting the staff and returning it to her holster at her back as she walked. She stopped and turned about the same distance from him as before. Nodding to Blaez, she said, "Whenever you are ready."

Blaez paced back and forth, hoping to take her by surprise by making it harder for her to time his attack. He took off like a shot toward her, and Maelona stood still, watching him. Then, when he was about to go in for the killing strike, with fangs bared and great paws reaching for her, she dodged to the side. She grabbed a handful of the fur on his shoulder and swung herself up onto his back. She locked one arm around his neck, and with the other hand she reached out and grabbed his jaw. She quickly used the leverage on his jaw to jerk his head around, almost to the point of doing real damage.

In this position, Maelona leaned forward, her mouth close to his ear. So Blaez heard her very clearly when she said, "Crack! I just broke your neck."

Blaez stopped moving, and Maelona jumped off his back,

moving into his line of sight. "That might not kill a shifter, but it will put him out of commission for a while," Maelona said. Then she asked, "Do you need another demonstration?"

Blaez huffed and shook his head.

"In that case, shift back to your human form, and we will practice some hand to hand combat."

Blaez shifted as he walked away toward the edge of the clearing where he had left his loose cotton pants. Maelona's eyes were drawn to his form as he walked - strong, well-muscled back, wide shoulders, and a light sheen of perspiration on his skin. Suddenly realizing - and a little surprised at - where her mind had gone, Maelona shook herself and drew her mind back to the task at hand.

Once Blaez had dressed, he walked toward Maelona once again. "I'm ready," he began, and the words were hardly out of his mouth when Maelona threw a punch at him. He instinctively blocked the punch and offered one in return.

Maelona blocked his punch but then unexpectedly turned into his body, pushing his punching hand out to the side and turning so that her back almost touched his chest as she brought her elbow up and around behind her, striking him in the jaw. She kept turning her body until she was behind him, where she hopped back a step and then moved forward again to add more force as she punched with both fists into his kidneys. While she knew this hurt him some, it was only enough to make it clear what the result would be. She could hit with much more power and do much more damage when she needed to.

Blaez spun around, punching at Maelona again, but she blocked again and somehow managed to grab his wrist, flip it over, and push up on his hand, thereby locking his wrist. Then she swung her body around again, keeping his hand pinned in hers until his elbow was locked and she was pushing him face first into the ground. Blaez had to either move where she was leading him or take the chance of having his arm broken or elbow joint damaged.

They continued this practice for some time, taking turns attacking and defending so that Maelona could ensure Blaez was learning these techniques as well. They interspersed this with kicking and striking practice in a sparring format.

In the final technique of the practice session, Blaez ended up flat on his back while Maelona straddled him, pinning his legs with her feet on his thighs and pinning his arms with her own. Maelona was stronger and more muscular than most females he knew, and the dense muscle made her heavier than most as well. Still, Blaez knew he could throw her off him easily.

But suddenly, as he looked up at her, he found he didn't want to. Instead, his body stilled as he gazed up at her. When Maelona looked down at him and saw the expression on his face, her own expression morphed from a mischievous grin into something more serious.

He was acutely aware of her lithe body pressed along his, the closeness of her lips to his own. It was as if, in that moment, something changed, sparked between them. Blaez closed his eyes as Maelona lowered her mouth toward his. He felt her breath on his lips as she slid her nose along his in an affectionate gesture.

He sensed Maelona pull back slightly, and he opened his eyes to see her looking down at him with genuine affection. Then suddenly, in his peripheral vision, he caught movement above and to the left of Maelona's head, and he turned slightly to see what it was.

All around them where they lay, it seemed that any loose objects that had been on the ground - pebbles, leaves, twigs, grass - were floating in the air. When Maelona realized what Blaez was looking at, she jumped up with a start. At the same time, all of the floating objects fell back to the earth.

Blaez could see that Maelona was upset by what had happened, and he wanted to comfort her. So, he stood and reached a hand out to her, saying, "It's okay Maelona. It was nothing dangerous. We're fine."

"No, it is not okay," Maelona said quietly while staring down at the ground. "This is why I try not to get too close to people. I can easily lose control over my magic in emotionally-charged situations. I can't help but worry that I will hurt someone I care about."

Blaez sensed a warmth spreading through him with the realization of how important their brief moment was to her, how it stirred her enough for this reaction and her implication that she cared for him. However, this new understanding was tempered by the knowledge that she was afraid of her powers and of losing control.

Blaez wanted to reassure her. He wished they could go back to a few moments ago when they were close, so he could hold her and comfort her. He knew she would not allow that with how she was feeling right now, though, so he just stood looking at her, not knowing what to say and wishing she would really let him in.

After a moment, Maelona turned and started walking out of the clearing. After a few steps, though, she hesitated. Turning to face him again, she said, "We meet with the protectors tonight. If they agree, we will start training with them tomorrow."

Chapcer 8

That evening, just prior to the appointed time, Blaez and Maelona met again in the clearing. Blaez did not want there to be any awkwardness between them, so he decided to address the moment they had shared.

"Maelona," he said in a soft but earnest voice as he approached her, "I believe it's clear from what happened earlier that I would be more than happy if we were to become more than friends, or partners and allies in times of battle. You are the most amazing female I have had the honor of knowing, and I would be proud to belong to you, to share my life with you.

"However, I do understand your feelings about such things, and your worries and fears. I do not want what may be happening between us to become a source of worry and anxiety as well. Please know that I will be whatever you need me to be. I will be with you through the good and the bad. I am not going anywhere, and I will be there to fight by your side."

Blaez noticed her expression warming after his short, sincere speech. She was just opening her mouth to respond to him when they were interrupted by the sound of voices. The protectors were arriving.

Blaez began introductions.

"This is Caellum, who you may remember from when we brought the prince. He was on patrol at that time." Caellum nodded to Maelona. "He is the alpha protector."

"This is Tangi," Blaez continued while nodding toward the shifter male with reddish-brown hair who had entered with Caellum. "He is Caellum's second in command." Maelona nodded to him in greeting. "Next to Tangi is Caer. She is third in command of the protectors."

Blaez introduced each of the other protectors as they entered the clearing behind their leaders. "These are Breoc and Manus," he said, "Brina and Andraste, two of our female protectors, Aengus and his twin, Ansgar and, finally, Caderyn."

As this last, tall, broad-shouldered protector was introduced, he nodded to Maelona and said with a smile, "You can call me Cade."

"Our final two protectors are still out on patrol," Blaez continued. "They are Anyon, who is Aengus and Ansgar's younger brother, and Renny, who is the other female of our group."

With the introductions complete, Maelona addressed the group.

"I thank you all for coming here this evening. Whether you are aware or not, war is on the horizon. As difficult as it may be to believe, it is possible that this war may make it here, inside the Sacred Forest."

There were a few expressions of disbelief at this, but the protectors quieted quickly.

"We will need as many allies as we can get to keep that from happening." Maelona added.

"How do you know this?" Asked the young shifter with messy, light brown hair that Blaez introduced as Breoc earlier.

"Well, for one thing, the injured man that we carried into the village, we rescued him from an attack by three demonkin," Blaez answered for her.

"Inside the Sacred Forest," Maelona added.

"That's not possible," Breoc countered.

"I assure you, it is," said Blaez. "I was there, and I was left with the disgusting taste of demonkin blood in my mouth to remind me that it did, in fact, happen."

After a few more expressions of disbelief, Maelona said, "We don't have the luxury of time for us to convince you of what we know to be true. Right now, we should discuss what we can do to protect against this new threat.

"I would like the protectors, and even the adolescent males and females of your pack who have yet to begin training, to train with us starting tomorrow. The youth may find themselves pulled into the fight whether they wish to be or not. They need to know how to protect themselves. I would ask that you, as the pack's protectors, form a plan to train and prepare them for what may come to pass.

"We only have a few more days before the prince is able to travel again," Maelona continued, "but in the meantime, I would like to leave your people with skills and knowledge that they can practice and hone after we are gone. Before we leave, however, we will be meeting with the sorceress, your pack leader Carasek, and several elders and tribe leaders from neighboring villages, as I just mentioned. Protector captains from each group will be invited as well. The sorceress has sent out emissaries from the pack to ask for their attendance. During that meeting, we will speak about what is happening in our realm and discuss what we need to do to prepare."

Breoc, who hovered close to Caellum, interrupted with a light scoff. "Caellum has almost four hundred years, and you look much younger and much less experienced. What makes you more qualified than he to teach us or lead us?"

"Hush, insolent pup!" said Caer. "Do you not know to whom you speak?"

Before he could respond, a calm, resonant voice answered from the other side of the clearing as a man walked steadily toward them. Blaez immediately recognized Carasek, their pack leader.

"You, my young pup," he began, "are addressing Maelona Sima, daughter of our sorceress, Ailla Melyonen, and Maddock Sima, who was a sorcerer and a leader among the seers. You may be too young to recognize the meaning of this yourself, but let me assure you that what she lacks in age, she more than makes up for in knowledge and ability."

"Carasek," Maelona said as she bowed her head to the elder and chief. "Thank you for coming. And I do not mind young Breoc's doubts and questions. After all, I prefer for my actions to speak louder than my parentage, and he has, as yet, nothing to place his faith in."

"Well said, young Maelona," Carasek responded. "Yet I do expect those who serve our people to show appropriate respect to others."

"As do I," Caellum added, looking Breoc in the eye. "It is very short-sighted to judge a being based on appearances," he told Breoc. "I hope this is not a mistake you will make in the heat of battle."

Looking back at Maelona, Caellum returned to the business at hand. "Please continue, Maelona," he said.

The next hour or so was spent discussing the training that would take place beginning the next morning. They also worked out a patrol schedule so that all the protectors could benefit without leaving the village with any gaps in its defenses.

When the talks had concluded for the evening, they headed out. Maelona turned to Blaez and said, hesitantly, "I have a favor to ask of you."

"Anything," Blaez replied. And he meant it. He trusted that she would never ask him for anything that he would not be willing to give.

"I need to do something that will leave me vulnerable. It will need to happen over the course of a night, and I need someone I trust to stand guard. I would like for this to take place tonight, but I realize you may not be able to arrange that on such short notice. If you need a day or two to make arrangements…"

"No, it's fine," Blaez interjected. "I have already discussed it with Ailla and the others, and we all agreed that what you and I have ahead of us is more important than any other job right now. My only concern, at this time, is to support you in whatever you need."

"Good," Maelona replied, nodding her head. "That is good. Meet me, then, at my hut at twilight. We will head out from there."

A couple of hours later, Blaez approached Maelona's dwelling. He noticed another animal hide stretched out on a frame of sticks and branches, in the same way that she had prepared the hide when they first arrived. A few feet away, in a patch of dwindling sunlight, Maelona stood removing pieces of dried meat from a contraption formed of a tripod of sticks attached by a rope at the top. It had switches running between the legs on which the meat had been hanging.

As he walked up behind her, Blaez greeted her with a grin, saying, "You're preparing for the long journey ahead, I see."

"Yes, and don't worry; I am preparing plenty for you as well." She turned to smile at him as she put the last of the dried meat into a leather pouch. It always struck him like a blow when she smiled her full-blown smile at him like that. Around others, she tended to be quiet and calm, and her smile was just a slight curve of her lips. It didn't make her seem unfriendly. Instead, he understood that she preferred to watch and listen rather than to speak. And when she did speak, her words tended to be of import. She missed nothing.

So, it made him feel special that she seemed to save her big smiles and playful banter for him, like they had a special bond. He knew, at least, that she was becoming quite special to him.

Maelona took her pouch of dried meat and placed it inside a small shed, which he figured she must have constructed herself since it hadn't been there the first time he came here to see her. When she was done, she turned to Blaez and asked, "Are you ready?"

Blaez gestured in front of himself, saying, "Lead the way."

They turned and headed out into the woods to the west of

the village. As they left, the sun lowering over the horizon looked as though it was peeking over the trees and reaching back up to paint the sky orange in its wake. Songs from the few birds who were not yet sleeping carried around them, lifting the spirits and adding to the sense of peace and tranquility.

They walked in silence at first, with Blaez following Maelona's lead. Then, after a while, Maelona asked, "So whose hut is it that they assigned me, anyway? I hope I didn't leave anyone homeless."

"No," Blaez replied. "It belonged to a young hunter, so it's fitting in a way since you are quite a hunter yourself." He smiled over at Maelona. "He mated a few months ago, and they needed a bigger living space since they were looking to start a family."

Blaez noticed Maelona's expression change suddenly to sadness. "What is it, Maelona?"

"It just hits me now and then," she replied, "especially when I think of children and families, how much we have at stake. How much will change if we fail."

"Have you foreseen what may happen?" He questioned.

"I have seen a few possibilities, yes. If we are successful, the way the realm's people interact with each other will be greatly improved." She said. "But if we fail –" She cut off her words as she swallowed back emotion and shook her head.

Blaez reached out and took her hand. Giving it a light squeeze, he said, "Well, we'll just have to make sure we don't fail, won't we?"

They continued in silence for some time. Blaez did not let go of Maelona's hand as they walked. He tried to tell himself that it was only to give her support, but if he were honest with himself, he knew it was more than that as well.

Eventually, Blaez spoke again. "Do you have the ability to shift into wolf form, Maelona?" he asked. Maelona turned to look at him, and suddenly he worried he should not have asked.

"I hope you are not offended by the question," he added, "but I have to admit that I have wondered about it often. You are half shifter, after all, and your parents were both formidable beings within their peoples. I know you have powerful seer abilities, so I wondered if you have any of the shifter abilities as well."

Maelona turned to look ahead again, then after a moment said, "I can. I have not tried it in years, however. I think that my psyche has somehow associated shifting with magic, and thus all that happened those many years ago. I had only shifted once or twice before the events that led me to leave the pack. I hope that, one day, I will feel comfortable enough to share my wolf with you."

They continued in relative silence for another half an hour, walking close to each other in the night that was brightened by the moon and the many stars in the clear sky. Blaez found himself glancing over to Maelona numerous times, taking in how her eyes shone in the moonlight, and how shadow and light played across her features. *She is quite a beautiful creature, magnificent to behold,* Blaez thought to himself.

Finally, Maelona stopped beside a grassy field at the bank of a river. "We are here," Maelona said as she turned to face Blaez. "Now, it's time for me to explain what will be happening and what I require of you."

Blaez nodded at her in encouragement, as she seemed a little nervous.

"I need to send a message out to the other seer champions and to the seer elders. This is not a common ability in our people. Having the ability to see things is much simpler than causing things to be seen. For the former, one must simply be open and let the energy and visions flow. We are mere vessels through which information passes. This is why we usually have visions while we sleep. Sending specific messages out to others and gaining specific information in return, however, requires intense focus and concentration, and uses up a lot of energy.

"Usually, one only hears of elders being capable of such things. There are those who believe that the fact that I can do this at such a young age is due to my parentage. There are others who believe it has to do with my own magic. I believe it's due to both of these things.

"Still," Maelona continued, "it is not an easy task for me. If I don't want it to only happen spontaneously, under times of great stress, then I need to focus on performing the task by essentially shutting out the outside world. Because of that, I'm left vulnerable. I could lock myself up in my hut, but the task is easier for me out in the open. Under a clear, moonlit night like tonight is even better. And the other worry is that I need to be uninterrupted until I wake on my own."

"I understand," Blaez replied. "I will ensure no one approaches."

"Good," Maelona responded. "Thank you." Then she walked a few feet away and lay down on her back so that she was partially obscured by the grass.

Blaez was careful to stay alert to any movement or sound around him as his attention was drawn to Maelona, lying in the grass. The temperature of the air around him seemed to rise a couple of degrees as he watched. After a few moments, the air seemed to charge with energy, and a low, pale-lavender-colored light seemed to emanate out from Maelona and head off in every direction.

He was mesmerized by the sight at first, but concern for her well-being had him focusing back on her face. Her expression was relaxed, peaceful and...vulnerable, once again reminding him of his task. So, he headed out to patrol the area, all the while ensuring he stayed close enough to reach her quickly should any trouble come around.

Maelona awoke around dawn the next morning. He knew she had been sleeping for at least part of that time, because a few hours after she began, the lavender light had dissipated. Yet, she still looked weary.

"Are you okay?" He asked her as he approached.

"Yes, I'm fine," She replied.

"Are you sure?" He asked. She simply nodded in response.

He brushed back some hair that had fallen over her forehead, and noticed the worry lines there. However, he wouldn't push her if she didn't feel like talking right now. Instead, he took her hand again and led her back the way they had come the night before.

A little later that morning, Maelona was having breakfast with her mother.

"Prince Gareth will be in acceptable condition to leave soon," Ailla said.

"Will he be ready in two days time?"

"Yes," Ailla replied. "But, Maelona, he will have to try to take it easy for at least the first few days."

"I understand."

"I've arranged for the meeting with the elders and tribe leaders to take place later today, in the evening hours." Ailla said. "You and Blaez will attend, of course. I have asked a few of the top-ranking protectors to be present as well."

"I hope the protectors will stay in human form and not talk of shifting." Maelona said.

"Of course. I have let all the others know that Prince Gareth will also be attending and that we have not yet informed him that we are shifters. As far as he knows at this point, we are human."

"And a seer," Maelona added. "Okay. Tonight, we will meet, tomorrow myself, Blaez and Gareth will prepare for our journey, and the next day we will depart for Eastgate. If we travel at a steady pace, we should arrive there before the attack begins."

"Don't forget, Maelona…"

"I know. It will be a steady pace, but not too fast for Gareth. We should still get there in time, if the universe wills it.

"Now, I must be off, or I'll be late for the training session with the protectors. We have precious little time to get them ready. I need to use every moment with them I can get."

Maelona met Blaez and the other protectors at the clearing she and Blaez had practiced at previously.

"Thank you all for coming," Maelona began. "I have already demonstrated to Blaez certain vulnerabilities and limitations that you may have in wolf form. Due to these limitations, and the fact that you are all already adept at fighting in wolf form, I would like to focus on fighting in your human forms. I am not saying your wolves' abilities cannot be used to your benefit. They most certainly can. What I am saying is don't depend solely on your wolf. Be unpredictable and be ready to use whatever advantages you have.

"Your wolf form may be able to overpower many of the realm's creatures, but certainly not all. You will not be able to depend on brute strength, claws, and teeth all the time. If your opponent outmanoeuvers you, or if you need to keep an opponent alive, these things will not help you.

"During these times, you will need to use your intellect. You may not have as much power behind you in your human form, but you will have more weapons, both lethal and non-lethal. Instead of just a great paw with claws, you now have fingers," – she demonstrated fingers to the eyes, spear hand to the throat, thumbs to the eyes – "and knuckles," -- she demonstrated with a finger-joint strike to the throat. She continued her list, demonstrating each item as she went along. "You have hammer fist, back fist, knife-hand strikes, wrist strikes, elbow strikes, shoulders, knee, shin, top of the foot, ball of the foot, knife-edge of the foot, heel of the foot, instep.

"You have all of these weapons at your disposal, so use them. If your arms are trapped, head-butt. If your upper body is occupied with blocking, strike out with the knee or foot. If your opponent is larger or stronger than you are in human form, then use his size against him. If he is running toward you, sword in the air, wait until he is almost in range to strike, then step off the line, striking to the side of the knee as he moves past."

"All of these things sound great, Maelona," Aengus said, "but this is not how we are accustomed to fighting. Do you really think we can become proficient enough to use these strategies in time?"

"For the most part," she responded, "the trick is to not overthink things. Don't tense up or panic. Just let your body relax and react naturally."

"Well, for us," Caer said, "reacting naturally would usually be reacting in wolf form."

"And that is why you must practice as much as you can in the time you have," Maelona responded. "You will need to repeat the movements as often as you can so that your body will learn what to do and will do it automatically. You are all warriors. You will adapt."

"Maybe you just want us in human form because you can't defeat us in wolf form," Breoc said.

Many of the protectors started to admonish Breoc, but Maelona raised her hand to silence them.

"Let's just get rid of any doubt right from the start, shall we?" she said. Turning to look at all of them, she said, "shift."

"Who?" Breoc asked.

"All of you."

The protector leaders looked as though they wanted to argue, but Maelona stood firm and looked them calmly, waiting.

The wolf shifters walked to the edge of the clearing and removed their clothing. Then they all shifted to wolf form.

"I want you to attack me as you would any enemy. As a pack. But remember, real warriors are not the same as prey. They will not run from you. You will need to confront them and, in this case, me, head on."

Maelona stayed in place, but turned a slow circle as they surrounded her. She watched their faces and their bodies for any sign of intent to attack. As she suspected, since he seemed to think he had something to prove, Breoc was the first to charge toward her.

Maelona waited until the last moment before moving.

Then she jumped diagonally forward, off his line of attack, and grabbed his fur as he passed. She used it to launch herself onto his back, as she had done before with Blaez. This time, however, they were in a pack, and another wolf came at her.

Grabbing the fur on Breoc's side once again, she swung herself down, and the other wolf's jaw clamped on Breoc's back, where she had been just a moment before. Breoc yelped, but Maelona knew he wasn't really hurt. Since this was their first practice, they wouldn't be attacking full force.

Wrapping her legs around Breoc's torso, she used his fur in her hands to reposition herself underneath him. With one hand, she then pulled the cylinder from its holder at her back. She pressed it to his chest above her, then she let herself drop. She continued to put pressure on the cylinder as he continued forward so that it traveled in a vertical line from his chest to his stomach. As soon as he cleared her, she rolled over and stood up.

"If that had been my knife, your guts would now be on the ground," she called after him.

She didn't have time to say anything else, however, before another wolf was upon her. It knocked her to the ground, but as she fell, she turned to land on her back and pushed the button to extend her staff. As the great wolf snapped at her, she shoved the staff into his mouth, locking his jaw open. Then, grabbing one of her daggers, she drew the hilt across his throat.

"I just slit your throat," she said, loud enough to be heard over the growls and heavy breathing of the wolves.

They continued like this, the wolves attacking, Maelona defending and counter-attacking, until she had demonstrated a killing or maiming blow on each. Then they all stood in place or paced slowly until they caught their breath.

"Any questions?" Maelona asked.

Snorts and head shakes were the response, so she said, "Then, please, shift back."

Once the wolves were in human form and clothed again, Maelona addressed the group.

"Blaez and I will be leaving for Eastgate in a couple of days, so we will use all the time we have this afternoon, until our meeting, practicing some techniques. We will meet again tomorrow for as much time as we can spare.

"You will start in pairs. Blaez and I will demonstrate first, since we have practiced some together before now, and you will watch. You will then take turns trying the techniques with your partner while I move amongst you to adjust as needed.

"Please, put forth your best effort. I would like to fit in some group practice as well. That way, you will have an idea about how to respond in human form should you be attacked by more than one enemy."

"Also," Blaez added, "you will need to teach these things to anyone capable of learning and to keep practicing them yourselves, after Maelona and I have gone, and until we all come together again at Eastgate."

"Well," Caellum said, clapping his hands together, "let's get started then."

Chapter 9

Later that evening, Maelona and Blaez walked together to the fire circle in front of the sorceress' sanctuary. On the way, they discussed the preparations they would need to undertake the next day for their coming journey.

"As a wolf shifter, I won't be able to carry much in the way of provisions." Blaez said. "If I need to shift, I will have to abandon anything I take."

"And that may be even truer than you know," Maelona said. "After tonight's meeting, I would like you to always stay in wolf form when we are around outsiders, including the prince, unless I ask otherwise."

"Well, that's the first time anyone has asked that of me," Blaez said. "Usually shifters pretend to be simple humans in front of outsiders, to protect our existence. How will we confer?" He asked.

"One advantage to you staying in wolf form," she explained, "is that people tend to not take care with their words in front of animals, but they would if they knew the animal was a shifter. I would like to use this advantage until we get to know Gareth better. I will ensure that we have time to ourselves when you can shift back so we can strategize."

Blaez looked pleased with the idea of having time to themselves. Maelona ignored this at the moment, however. She figured she would deal with it when the time came.

"It never hurts to have the element of surprise and some

tricks on your side. I may have a surprise or two myself," she added. Blaez quirked a brow at this.

"We are here. I guess we will talk again later," Blaez said as they arrived.

Keeping to the shadows, Blaez removed his pants and put them in the rock alcove. He shifted, and Maelona ran her hand through the fur between his ears. He pushed his head into her hand in response. Then, they went to take their places next to Ailla and Prince Gareth.

All around the fire circle, elders and protectors from their own village, as well as those from any other villages within a few days' travel, talked quietly and solemnly. Maelona and Blaez were the last to arrive. Once they did, Ailla made introductions around the circle.

When they were seated, Maelona lifted her face to the sky and looked up at the myriad of bright stars shining above them. She closed her eyes and took a deep breath, calming and opening her mind for what was to come. She lowered her head again and sat in quiet contemplation as Ailla began to speak.

"There are countless histories and oral traditions that many of our peoples share. Some of these are tales meant to scare children into behaving. Some serve as a warning of very real dangers before we encounter them. Some are as old as time, some are true accounts of things that have come to pass, and some tell of what is yet to come.

"It is said that our world was created to be in balance. Light and darkness, youth and agedness, beauty and ugliness, goodness and evil. There are those species that were created to be evil, such as the demonkin and some of the shifter species. There are others who are created to be good, such as certain other animal shifters, including the dragons, who are known to be very rigid in their views of right and wrong. There are also species that are neither good nor evil, such as the elves and the humans, who tend to do things for the furthering of their own people, or of themselves.

"Of course," Ailla continued, "as all beings are free to make their own choices, there are exceptions to this structure. There are histories, for example, of a demonkin male who went out of his way to try and help some travelers in need, despite the disregard this earned him in his own clan.

"Because of these shared histories, all the youth of the realm, regardless of which species they are a part of, have heard the stories of the great war between good and evil that took place over a fifty-year period a few thousand years ago. Of course, the versions of the stories that are told vary greatly from species to species." The sorceress laughed lightly with a slight shake of her head.

"What the elders and wise men of all the peoples know to be true, however, and what they guard as a secret passed down to their successors, is what caused this war, and what came to pass because of it." She paused and looked around at the elders, who nodded solemnly.

"In the center of our realm, and spanning a huge distance, there are ley lines that join together roughly in the shape of a diamond. From each axis, more ley lines spread inwards, until they meet in the middle.

"These ley lines surge with magical energy. Any sorcerer, at any time, at any ley line, and at any point along the line, can use this energy to bolster their magical abilities. Where the lines join at the axes, this magical energy is even stronger. In the center, where they all meet, the magical energy is so strong that many sorcerers have been destroyed trying to access it."

Ailla paused a moment before continuing. "A few millennia ago, there was a powerful sorcerer who called himself Anceannmor. He had dedicated his life to learning how to use this source of magic and thereby gain power and dominion over all the peoples of the realm. Eventually, he discovered that when the stars and planets align in a certain configuration, it causes an interesting effect on the hub where the ley lines from the axes join. During the alignment, the powerful and unstable magical energy found at this hub becomes focused and stable enough to use without the user being destroyed, despite its great strength during this time.

"Anceannmor found a way to use the surge of magical energy

at the hub to open a gate to another realm, a realm where evil dwells. He hoped to create and lead an army of demons, which he would use to help destroy our realm's leaders and to subjugate our peoples. His plan seemed to work, for a while.

"Soon, the evil beings he had brought over turned on him as well, as such is the way of evil. The chaos this caused created an opportunity for the sorcerers of the light to combine their power in an alliance that allowed them to sweep in and push the demons back through the gate. During the Battle of the Gate, it is believed that Anceannmor was destroyed. The sorcerers of the light then closed the gate and locked it with magic. Once closed, it could not be reopened until the stars and planets align once more, thereby stabilizing the power of the hub enough to use once again. As powerful as they were, none of the sorcerers at that time had the power or knowledge needed to destroy the gate completely.

"This conflict was the beginning of the War of Fifty Years."

After a pause, during which those present continued to sit silent and transfixed, Ailla carried on. "Some demons were left behind and began breeding with the human inhabitants of the northern mountains. The demonkin are not native to our realm, as many now believe. These dark inhabitants of our realm are in fact descendants of the stranded demons left behind. These creatures thought that if they banded together, they would be powerful enough to continue Anceannmor's plans for domination of the realm.

"The part of this history that has been passed down through the years since, in one form or another, tells of how these demons gathered supporters from some of the realm's peoples by playing on greed and using manipulation. Many saw these machinations for what they were and resisted. The result was a war of numerous battles and sieges, and many deaths, that lasted fifty years before the forces of good were finally successful in pushing back these interlopers and would-be subjugators. The demonkin now occupy an area up past the Thuaidh Mountains, way up north where the terrain is cold, harsh, and unforgiving. We rarely see or hear from them anymore to the south of that mountain range."

Gareth spoke first following Ailla's recounting of history. "The castle town of Eastgate, where my father, King Niall, rules, has recently been under attack. So far, it has just been small scale, as if they are testing our defenses. When I came here into the Sacred Forest, I was followed and attacked by what I now know were three demonkin." There were several gasps and murmurings around the fire circle when he said this. "After my attack, and your story," Gareth continued, "I think it's likely that demonkin are behind the attacks on the town as well. What I want to know now is what this history lesson has to do with the recent goings-on at Eastgate? And how do we even know if it *does* have to do with the goings-on at Eastgate? Could it just be a coincidence?" he asked.

"Here, I will defer to Maelona," the sorceress replied, "as the answer falls within her area of expertise."

Maelona began speaking to the group in a soft, calm voice that resonated for all to hear.

"As some of you know, I have come here from the seer village." At this, there were some mumblings, and even a couple of gasps. Seers were considered an almost-extinct race that rarely showed themselves, even among the magical beings of the realm.

"For some time," Maelona continued, "...years, even, my people have received visions of an evil that has been covertly trying to insinuate its way throughout the realm. Almost all the human peoples have been affected in some way or other. The evil creeps in subtly, pretending to be a friend, while manipulating the thoughts and hearts of the people, playing on their fears and insecurities, and using their greed against them.

"For years, the seers have worked to try to cut off this evil influence when possible and to learn as much as we can. For the past three-hundred years, this work has been as unobtrusive as possible." Here, Maelona paused for a moment before continuing.

"Several months back, information came to us that strongly suggested that these were the same evil forces that had begun the fear-mongering that led to the near extinction of the seer people. Since this has come to our attention, our people have received more and more visions of war and violence, fire and pain. We believe these evil forces were trying to rid the world of seers so that they could keep the element of surprise on their side. And of course, our natural abilities would also make us a considerable force on the side of good. We believe, as well, that these same forces were responsible for the destruction of the dragons a century before that. Like they were trying to rid the world of the biggest threats to their plans."

"Couldn't this all be coincidence?" one of the elders asked. "After all, we are talking about events that occurred centuries apart, even millennia if we look back to the Battle of the Gate. What are the chances that these are all related, really?"

"It could be coincidence, it's true," Maelona responded. "However, some of us seers have been having visions that show glimpses of these events, one right after the other. Sometimes they all repeat again, in the same order, in succession. This strongly suggests that they are linked.

"It is true that the same people who started it all would be dead by now, but we believe it may be some cult or following of Anceannmor, or of the original demons, that have been following a long-plan of disintegration of our defenses over the years."

"So, what is their plan? What do they want?" A voice from the crowd asked.

"They want the same thing any war-mongering beings want: power, wealth, subjects to bow at their feet." Maelona said. "The real fear is that the leader himself wants more than this. Our visions lead us to believe that he wants to subjugate or enslave all the peoples of Sterrenvar, and proclaim himself leader over us all."

"Surely this being must be greatly overestimating his abilities." The same voice from before said. "There is no one person in the realm with enough power to do that, is there?"

"Unfortunately," Maelona replied, "if what our visions suggest is true, then there is a very powerful sorcerer leading the cause. And his followers believe in him enough to want to be part of the world he wishes to create. So, yes, there is someone who potentially has enough power to follow through with this plan."

"So, why the history lesson," Gareth asked her. "How is what happened three-thousand years ago linked to what is happening now?"

"Again, from what we've seen in our visions, we believe this present-day sorcerer wishes to follow in Anceannmor's footsteps and use the great gate to create an army to take over the realm, or at least to bolster the army he has already created. He may even be a disciple of Anceannmor's. It is possible that we are wrong, of course, as our visions don't show us everything and have not been clear of late. However, the stars will soon be once again aligned as they were almost three-thousand years ago. It is unlikely that a sorcerer with aspirations of leading the realm would let such a significant event pass on without trying to use it to their advantage. After all, they would have to wait another three-thousand years for such an opportunity to come again."

Brennus, the young, dark-haired, dark-eyed leader of a neighboring wolf shifter pack to the south spoke up in an agitated voice, "This is all very fascinating. And horrifying. But how do your visions help us? Do they tell us whether we are to be victorious or not? Do they show us *how* to be victorious? How to rid this evil from the world?"

"Our visions have shown us the attack of the Great Gate, and how the dark sorcerer will seek to destroy the keystones," Maelona said. "Our original plan was for the seer champions and gate kings to protect the keystones and gather allies to go to the Great Gate to take a stand. We figured that if the keystones held strong, our enemy would not be able to get the power boost they needed to open the Great Gate."

"Okay, back up," Gareth said. "Keystones? What are these keystones?"

"I will explain that in a moment, once Maelona has finished her part," Ailla said.

"These demonkin in our forest," Maelona continued, "this really worries me. It leads me to believe he is pushing forward the 'take over the realm' part of his plan much sooner than expected."

"Or he could be trying to distract us," Carasek said.

"Why would he be trying to distract us," Brennus asked,

"when it is the humans he is targeting? We are not allies. Most of the humans don't even believe we exist anymore."

"I know I didn't," Gareth said. "Apparently, we've been blind fools."

"We need to be their allies whether they acknowledge us or not," Maelona said. "If you think for one moment he will be satisfied with taking over only the human parts of the realm, then you underestimate the megalomaniacal mind.

"Your point is valid, though. He would not assume we would be jumping in to aid the humans at this point, I don't think."

"Either he is very powerful indeed," Taranis, the dignified and impressive king of the golden eagle shifters, said, "or he is very arrogant."

"Let us hope it is arrogance," Ailla added, "for arrogance can cause a foe to greatly overestimate their own chances and underestimate their opponents. It can be their downfall."

"Then, yes, let's hope that it is arrogance," Brennus agreed.

Chapter 10

Carasek, their own pack's alpha, had been silent to this point. Now he stood and addressed the group. "As Maelona has explained to us before," he began, glancing in her direction, "people have free will and decisions can be changed. The future is never set in stone. But the seers can provide us information on past and current actions, intentions, and many other things that would be invaluable for us to know as we prepare for the dark times to come."

"How do we know that she can be trusted?" Brennus questioned. "How do we know she is not working with the evil forces, trying to lure us in and make us vulnerable? After all, we have no proof of what she claims she sees."

"I realize that some people still live with the unfounded fear and suspicion that had been tacked to the seer name many years ago," Carasek said. "But you should remember that the same suspicion and fear was turned on us after the seers disappeared. If I were a betting man, I would wager that this was a fabrication created to cause a divide between our peoples; a rift to weaken the strength we have when we band together. The information the seers can provide could mean the difference between success and failure, victory and defeat. And I for one will take the gift of their friendship and support with grace and gratitude, as will my pack."

Maelona was aware of the residual negative opinions toward the seer people left over from all those years ago, and she was accustomed to it. However, she wanted to clarify a few truths for those present. After all, it would be unwise to try to work with supposed allies who did not trust you. The falsehoods spread by evil mouths about her people had bred mistrust and caused distrust between not only the humans and the seers, but between all the peoples of the realm for the past three-hundred years.

In that moment, she decided it needed to end. So, she spoke up.

"I know what many of you think of the seer people," she began in a calm and steady voice. "But let me inform you of our truth."

"At the very core of our belief system is the knowledge that we were created for a purpose. That we were given the advantages we have for a reason. We were created to protect our realm and all the people in it. Otherwise, why would our visions always point us to where we are needed most? To where evil and danger threaten good people?

"There was a time when all of the people of the realm mingled together and co-existed peacefully. Then three-hundred years ago – longer when you look at what happened with the dragons – an evil force began lurking behind the scenes, fearmongering, twisting truths into ugly lies about my people.

"But I want you all to think on something," she said, her voice intense. "Do you really believe that the seer people, with all our advantages, could have been slaughtered by humans and demonkin if we had fought back?

"My people trusted too much that the humans would make the right choice. Then, when it became evident that they chose wrongly, many seers saw the humans as victims who were being manipulated and used as tools by those who wished to eradicate us. But make no mistake. We have learned from our past, and we will defend ourselves if such a thing were to happen again."

"At least your people learned you are not all-powerful," called another voice from the crowd.

"We never said we were," Maelona said. "We never pretended to be anything other than what we are."

Maelona shook her head. "Human lives are short; thus,

their collective memories are short. So, to a degree, they can be forgiven for forgetting who we are. The real disappointment came when the longer-lived, magical races of the realm started to believe the evil whispers as well.

"You know us. At least, you knew us. You should have known better.

"The reason, I think, that it was so easy to believe the lies is because they were so close to the truth. We do intrude on people's privacy, though not intentionally. We do manipulate, but only to counteract evil's manipulations. However, contrary to what you were led to believe, we do not get to chose who, where, or when we see. We see only what the universe sends us, and it only gifts us visions of where darkness and evil threaten. The universe shows us where we are needed most.

"And right now, we are needed to help bring the realm's peoples together to stand against what is perhaps the most powerful dark sorcerer our realm has ever known."

When she was finished, she was trembling. She felt Wolf press up against her, offering her support, which she gladly accepted.

After a pause, during which there was a quiet stillness around the fire circle, Caellum spoke up. "We would be living our lives in ignorance of the dangers heading for us if not for the seers. We would be easy targets."

"So, enlighten us, seer," Brennus said, causing Blaez to growl at him once again, "what could give us an advantage over these insidious evil forces?"

Maelona had looked across the fire circle at Brennus as he spoke, and she could see in his eyes and face that his brashness signified true concern for his people. She continued to look at him with a seemingly impassive expression until she caught his gaze. As they looked at each other, Maelona knew that despite his bold and forward ways, he was a man who could be trusted.

Everyone had been still during this silent exchange, waiting to see what would happen. There seemed to be a collective release of breath as Maelona shifted her gaze from Brennus to look around the circle once again. She nodded to Ailla, who stood up to add the next information.

"When the sorcerers of the light defeated Anceannmor and his demons," Ailla began, "they knew they had to do something to protect against such a thing happening again. So, they created four keystones, imbued with strong, positive magical energy, and placed them at the four axes of the ley lines. They are meant to inhibit any dark magic from flowing through and, in particular, to interrupt the flow of magic to the hub. They do not stop the flow of magic completely. Rather, the intent was to create an obstacle or deterrent. If the keystones would not stop the flow of magic completely, they would at least lessen it and, hopefully, buy time to stop any evil forces from using it to compromise or destroy our realm.

"As you all know, there are four major kingdoms in our realm: Northgate, Eastgate, Southgate, and Westgate. These kingdoms were given those names for a reason. Each of these kingdoms was founded on an axis of the ley lines. Each castle is found in the center of its town, which is surrounded by high, stone walls. The castles themselves have highly trained elite guards constantly watching for danger. In the very center of each castle, and partly constructed underground, there are highly fortified and magically shielded keeps, and within each keep there is a keystone."

Maelona stood up at this point, adding, "Ever since The War of Fifty Years, the seer people have appointed four seer champions. There are also trainees preparing to take our places should we become unable to fulfill our duties. Each champion is entrusted with watching over one of the gates and its keystone. We travel far and wide as well, watching and listening to discern any threat to the well-being of the realm. Though we look for any hints of this evil returning, our main responsibility is protecting the keystones. If any of us should fail, or if the danger is great enough, we will band together to protect the Great Gate, which Anceannmor built over the hub of the ley lines."

Taranis spoke up again. "Might I ask," he began in a deep and rumbling voice, "for some clarification here? You are concerned with protecting the keystones, and the Great Gate, yet you have also said that only a powerful sorcerer could access the power of the hub. Do we know if the keystones reduce the power at the hub enough so that beings with less powerful magic can access it? Or, are you assuming that there is a sorcerer with for-midable abilities who has made an alliance with the demonkin?"

After a brief moment of hesitation, Maelona answered Taranis' question. "Magical defenses were placed at the hub after the Battle of the Gate, in the hopes of deterring those of weaker magical power from trying to access it. As for whether there is a sorcerer involved, we do not need to assume anything.

"For the past couple of years, my people and I have had visions of what is to come, as well as visions of what is going on elsewhere in the present. These visions have become more frequent and more insistent for the past couple of months. However, we have yet to receive anything clear on who is behind what is happening. This, in itself, is evidence that there is a pow-erful sorcerer who is having some success at making visions of himself - or herself - quite hazy."

Maelona and Ailla looked at each other in silent communi-cation, and then Ailla took up the task of information-sharing. "We may not know for certain who is behind everything. We do not have solid proof that it is a sorcerer, but the seers' visions, or holes in their visions, rather, strongly suggest this to be so.

"Furthermore, we do know that in forty days the stars and planets will once again be aligned as they were three millennia ago, and the power at the hub will once again be vulnerable to attack and use by those with less than noble intentions. And only a sorcerer could use this advantage."

At this information, the rumblings of concerned voices filled the air until a voice spoke up above the crowd, asking, "Do you believe the keystones will be enough to stop this sorcerer from opening the gate?" All fell silent to hear the response.

"Honestly," Maelona replied, "until we know more about who this dark sorcerer is, we cannot say for certain. We believe they will be enough, but if even one of us four champions should falter…"

"What would we do," the same voice in the crowd asked, "if one of you should fail in protecting the keystones, or the key-stones should fail to work as hoped?" The rumblings through the crowd picked up again, this time with a hint of panic.

"The answer to your question," Maelona began, and the crowd became quiet as she spoke, "will also answer Brennus' previous question, I believe.

"About a millennium or so after The Battle of the Gate, a powerful seer sorceress named Scota helped direct our people, alongside the elders of the time. She was strong and fearless, with her martial skills rivaling her magic.

"Scota had visions of this battle we will soon be facing. Unfortunately, the information she left us tells us no more than what we have seen about the dark sorcerer himself, or herself. However, she also foresaw the coming of a powerful magical… article into our possession. She saw how this magical article could be used to stop the gate itself from opening and to hold back the demonkin from invading our realm. Scota referred to this item as the Ternias."

At this point, Ailla interjected, looking to Maelona with a concerned countenance. "There is much danger involved with the use of the Ternias, however, so we plan to use it only as an absolute last resort." She spoke these last few words with force and determination.

"How do we locate this Ternias and how is it used?" Taranis asked. "My kind has unrivaled sight, even at great distances, and our gift of flight helps us to travel much faster than most. May the eagle shifters offer you assistance?"

"My thanks to you, Taranis," Ailla replied. "We will be in great need of your help in the coming months, and I thank you for your kind offer. Luckily," she continued, "the Ternias was located some years back and is in our possession as we speak. We will need all the help we can get in the battles to come, yet only one is capable of carrying the Ternias to the gate and wielding it in battle. And that is my own daughter, Maelona."

Once again, a murmuring arose between those seated around the circle.

"No offense meant to your daughter, Sorceress," Brennus said, "but Maelona is still young. Are you sure she is the best choice to take on such an important task?"

Caellum now spoke up again. "Maelona has been training with our protectors and trainees - in fact, she has been *training* us. Most of us are quite experienced fighters, yet none of us could take her down. She has taught us many skills that I am certain will be highly useful in the battles to come. I can assure you, Brennus, and any other among you who may doubt her capability, that what she may lack in age compared to many of our fighters, she makes up for in martial arts skill, tactical knowledge, intuition, and wisdom. My protectors and I would be proud to follow her into battle."

Looking at those gathered around the circle, Maelona could tell that many of those who had not previously known her were affected by this show of faith and loyalty. She was very touched by Caellum's words herself, and she hoped she could live up to them.

"Thank you very much for your words of support, my dear Caellum," said the sorceress. Turning to address Brennus and the others once again, she added, "However any of you feel about this *choice*, know that there truly is no choice. As I said before, Maelona is the only one who can bear the Ternias. And, once again, I truly hope it will not get to that point."

Taranis then asked, "So tell us, Maelona, what is your plan? What do you need us to do?"

Maelona gestured at the prince, saying, "I foresaw that Prince Gareth would head for the Glenn Shelladah, the Valley of Sight, in search of the seer village... and my father. However, I also foresaw that his presence would be needed at this meeting, and so I remained here waiting and preparing. One night I had a vision of him in a dream. He was being attacked by demonkin not far from here, as he has already spoken about. So, I headed out to meet him, and found him in the thick of a battle with three demonkin."

"Demonkin? In the Sacred Forest?" said a protector from the neighboring pack. "I heard him when he said it, but I was hoping he had misspoken." Other voices joined in agreement.

Once the chatter had lessened a little, Maelona continued, confirming, "Yes, demonkin in the Foraoise Naofa. I believe their mission was to prevent Gareth from seeking help. That way the coming danger would continue moving forward, unknown to us, for as long as possible. The attacks at Eastgate are tied to what has been happening around the realm, and to what will happen at the Great Gate. It would seem that the demonkin are as misinformed about the seer presence and influence as most others in the realm," she said.

"Gareth had come looking for my father," Maelona continued, "in the hopes of finding help for the danger to his own father and kingdom that have been making themselves known of late. Of course, in my father's absence, the task falls to me.

"The attack on Gareth and the threats to the security of Eastgate tell us that whoever is behind the plot is worried enough about the keystones to try and take them out first, which means our first action will be to travel to Eastgate to protect the keystone found there, as originally planned. The three other seer champions are either already at their assigned gates, or they are on their way. We have been tasked to try and gather support in the form of allies on the way to guard our gate, which is why you are all here tonight."

"Maelona and I," Ailla said, "along with our pack's protectors, have been trying to analyze their actions thus far, and to postulate what their next move may be. We believe the demonkin, as well as the force that leads them, are trying to weaken the defenses at Eastgate and to make the city's defenders nervous so that they make mistakes. We do not believe, however," she continued, "that the main attack at the Great Gate will occur for a few weeks yet.

"The sorcerer behind all this is cunning, and so we must assume he would want to wait as long as possible to attack the Gates. We think that he would want to wait long enough so that we would not be able to fix any damage to the keystones before the attack on the Great Gate, but with enough time for them to withdraw and return to him again should he need it."

Taranis, who was no stranger to battles and battle plans, joined in at this point. "If we provided a strong enough defense to protect the keystone, or if we weakened his army enough, then his plan would be moot."

"Yes, this is true, and that is what we hope to accomplish with this meeting tonight – by bringing our peoples together," Maelona replied. "We need to join together to create a force formidable enough to withstand the attack at the Great Gate and to beat back the demonkin hoard." After pausing in thought for a moment, she continued, "In fact, if we could make swift enough work of the demonkin at the gate-towns, we could head to the Great Gate as soon afterward as possible. If chance is on our side, we may find the sorcerer behind the mayhem there, and put an end to him once and for all."

"Is that really necessary if we are successful in protecting the keystone? Won't that neutralize the threat?" Brennus asked for clarification.

"My dear Brennus," Ailla replied, "it is not just 'necessary'; it is vital.

"Though the seers can contact each other from time to time, this is difficult to do and would be almost impossible in the heat of battle. So, we may not know for some time if the other keystones have fallen or remain firm. Also, the magic of the keystones, and of the protective spells at the Gate itself, are old and untested. We do not know how effective they will be, especially since we do not yet know exactly how powerful our enemy sorcerer is. We can only hope for the best, but we must plan and prepare for other possibilities."

"Also, you all have seen how this evil lurks, poisons, and builds behind the scenes," Maelona added. "If we do not cut the poison from the flesh once and for all, it will grow again in time."

"Even if we do defeat this evil sorcerer, some other evil being will just rise to take his place," Gareth commented.

Carasek responded, "The less evil in the world the better if you ask me."

"We also have an advantage over the demonkin and their leader," Ailla added, as she looked to Maelona with a smile. "They hope to have the element of surprise on their side, but they have no idea of the number of seers and the breadth of their influence. Because of the seers, we have much information that we would otherwise not be privy to. We all should be grateful to the seer people for their insight and protection, for without it, there would be little hope for victory."

"There is something you are overlooking, though," Taranis added. "If the dark sorcerer is taking the energy to interfere with the seers' visions, he must believe there is the possibility that there are still some seers in existence. We need to be careful."

Many voices sounded out in agreement from around the fire circle.

"This is true," Maelona said. "But even if they did believe there were many of us left, they do not know for certain. In my opinion, though, even more important than the seer presence is the fact that the demonkin and their dark sorcerer will not be expecting us all to be fighting side by side. They will not be expecting the magical beings of the realm to be fighting as allies to the humans.

"Our largest advantage will be our ability to put aside old prejudices to stand side by side against them."

There were a couple of shouts of agreement at this, and Maelona took a moment to look around at those gathered. There were some who sat quietly, seeming lost in thought. There were some who talked together seriously. There were still others who spoke excitedly about what was to come. Then, there were some who were looking at her, to her, as if awaiting her next words of wisdom and guidance.

Maelona quickly looked away from those gathered, and back to her mother and Carasek. She nodded her thanks to them for the show of support today. Internally, however, the more faith people proclaimed to have in her, the more anxious she became. She hoped she was strong enough to follow the path laid before her to its very end, whatever it may be.

Chapter 11

The next morning, Blaez arose early to prepare for the journey ahead. Of course, like most shifters, he preferred to travel light. He had a pack he could wear in human form, but as a wolf, he would have to carry it in his mouth. Being burdened in this way was not convenient when hunting or fighting, so it would often have to be left somewhere to be retrieved later.

He had just gathered a few items together and laid them out on his bed when he heard a knock. "Enter," he called, and he turned to see Maelona in the doorway. "Maelona," he greeted as he nodded to her. "I wasn't sure I would see you before this afternoon's practice since you have your own preparations to make."

"I do," Maelona replied. "However, I have brought some things that may help you with your packing."

She took a bundle of folded, softened leather out of her pack and laid it on the bed. Then she picked up each piece, one at a time, and explained it to him.

"This is a pair of pants, similar to my own, that lace up on the outer side of each leg. This is useful for size changes in time of feast or famine, and it makes them quick to remove when necessary." Blaez took the pants from her and marveled at the smooth feel of the soft, brown leather in his hands.

"The extra benefit to you is that the leather of the pants is supple yet strong, and I have reinforced the eyelets. If you must suddenly switch to your wolf form, you may need to replace the laces, but the pants themselves should remain intact." With a smile, she added, "I put extra laces in the pack."

Blaez wondered about this pack she mentioned, but before he could ask, Maelona held up another article of clothing. "This vest is similar to mine as well. It is laced in the front, again with the benefit of being able to tighten or loosen it as needed, within reason. Obviously, I would not be able to don your vest and expect it to fit." Again, she smiled at Blaez, but he had no words at that moment.

She continued, "Unlike my vest, your vest has laces down the sides underneath the arms. This way, it won't be shredded at the shoulders and sides with a quick shift." Smiling at him again, she added, "I put *many* extra laces in the pack." Blaez loved the look of mirth that shone on her face as she said this.

Blaez suddenly realized that Maelona was talking much more than usual, and much faster. She must be nervous, and his lack of response could not be helping. He should say something to ease her nervousness. Before he could, however, Maelona continued with her instruction.

"Then there is the pack itself. It is similar to my own," she said while gesturing to the pack on her back. To demonstrate, she quickly unfastened the waist strap and swung it around to her front, where she could easily access the contents. "You should try it."

Blaez stood there, overwhelmed by her gifts and not knowing how to respond. This pack…it was almost as if she had read his mind. So, as he stayed frozen in place, Maelona took the pack, reached up, and slid the chest strap over his head. He ducked a little to aid her. Then she reached around his waist with both hands to grab the waist strap.

They both paused as they realized how close together this maneuver had brought them. It was almost as if she were embracing him. Blaez could not help but notice that Maelona simply paused - she did not tense up or show any discomfort at this closeness. Then, she slowly pulled back to fasten the waist strap. Blaez was aware that she inhaled deeply as she moved, breathing in his scent.

Once the strap was secured, Maelona looked up into Blaez's

eyes, raising her hand to cup his cheek. Blaez felt his heart race at the feel of her warm hand on his face.

It was not a soft hand. Instead, it was the strong and calloused hand of one who worked and fought hard. Yet somehow, her touch was warm and feminine. He felt hope welling inside him, but he knew Maelona had to lead, that she had to be ready.

"My mother has been helping me practice my magic," Maelona said softly as she held his gaze. "She believes that I need to stop trying to control it. That I need to accept it as part of myself and let it flow freely." Her gaze turned earnest as she continued, "I want to try, but you must understand that I have been focusing on controlling my emotions and my magic for so long…this will be an ongoing process for me. Already, though, I have felt more open and carefree with you than I have with anyone else for many years."

She held his eyes with her own, and Blaez knew she was trying to get him to understand something important. And he did. He knew that she was not just referring to her sorcery practice. He knew that things had to progress slowly, that Maelona needed to dictate the pace.

Blaez was already sure of his feelings for her. Therefore, although it might be difficult for him to hold himself back, he would commit to giving her whatever she needed.

He nodded slightly and said, "I will give you whatever you need from me, my Lona. You need never doubt me." With these words of reassurance, Maelona pulled him down to her to kiss him softly, then pulled back slightly to look at him again. Blaez could see something spark to life in her eyes, as if the brief contact had awakened something inside her. He felt it too. She pulled him to her again, this time bringing him in for a deeper kiss, which he returned with equal passion.

Blaez knew she was beginning to fully let go and let herself just be in the moment when she pressed her form up against his own. As their tongues met in an intricate dance, Blaez suddenly felt all the hair on his body stand on end, as if the air was filled with an electrical charge. While it did pull them out of the moment, unlike that day in the meadow, she did not jump back suddenly in surprise. Instead, she pulled back slowly, reluctantly, and the electrical charge gently dissipated as she did so.

"Ahem," she said and looked down to the floor. After a moment, she declared, "We had better get back to the task at hand."

Maelona continued with her instructions in the same matter-of-fact fashion as before. Blaez figured she was trying to ignore or alleviate any awkwardness after what had just happened.

"This pack is easily adjustable and easy to remove. I have added twice the length to the straps than I would have normally used to accommodate your additional size when you shift. You just need to grab hold here," she took his left hand and guided it to the chest strap, "and here," and she took his right hand and guided it to the waist strap. "Then you just lift the clasps and pull outward."

Guiding Blaez's hands with her own, she demonstrated lifting and pulling on both straps at the same time, in one swift movement. The straps slipped out until the ends caught on loops so that they were now much looser than they had been just a short moment ago.

"Once you become accustomed to the movement, it should take only a fraction of a moment to accomplish. To tighten them again when you shift back, you grab here," she grabbed the ends of the straps, now at the loops, "and pull them back until they are snug once again, and you push the clasps back into position." Blaez noticed this was adjustable as well, with a few places to attach each clasp.

When Maelona was finished with the demonstration, she removed her hands from his, stepped back, and looked at Blaez uncertainly, almost nervously. "What do you think? Do you think it will work for you?" she asked. "I know I asked you to stay in wolf form as much as possible, but there will be times when you will go in human form as well. You will need to have clothing with you, as many of the human villages are not as accepting of nudity as shifters are…although, I am sure the human females would enjoy the spectacle," she added with a smirk. Then she looked at him expectantly while awaiting his response.

It took Blaez a few moments to find his voice, despite

Maelona's attempt at lightening the moment. Not wanting her to worry, however, he leaned in and kissed her softly. He felt a little overwhelmed…happy, but overwhelmed with physical and emotional sensation. He may have longed for it since shortly after they met, but this was the first time that Maelona had laid her hands on him outside of sparring. And it was definitely the first time she had kissed him.

More than that, however, he was touched by her gifts, which he knew she had made with her own hands.

"These gifts for me are what you have been working on this whole time with the tanning of the deer hides, are they not?" Maelona nodded.

"The time you must have put in, not to mention the thought and labor involved in creating items of such practicality and craftsmanship…"

Maelona shrugged and responded, "I used the hide of the stag we hunted together for the majority of it until it ran out. Then I hunted another deer to complete it.

"Back in the seer village," she said, "family and close friends customarily employ their best skills to create useful gifts for those who set out on dangerous journeys. In fact, the more useful and well thought-out the gift, the higher the esteem. That is how I came to possess the weapons I currently carry, in fact."

"Oh, yes?" Blaez teased. "And who made your gifts? Should I be worried?"

Maelona let out a short burst of laughter. "Not at all," she said. "I have no brother, but Anwyl is the closest one can come when there is no blood relation."

Blaez looked at the items again in awe. "I would normally pay dearly at the marketplace to buy such items, but they wouldn't be so carefully thought out. How is it our own artisans haven't thought of these designs?"

"Well, they have not had the need, not really," Maelona responded. "After all, for the last three centuries, the shifters, like the seers and most of the other magical beings who inhabit the Foraoise Naofa, have limited any contact with those living outside our beloved forest. And when we do make our way into their towns and villages, it's always in human form. It has gotten so that, for some of the outlying human territories, we have become little more than the stuff of legends and fairy tales." Blaez quirked a brow in surprise.

"So, you wouldn't have needed to shift as often, and the shifters tend to not care about nakedness. You, however, will be visiting villages and towns with me so you will need such things." Maelona continued, "I want you to be prepared. We seers and, in particular, the seer champions, wear clothing made this way because it is very useful to us. While slipping in and out of villages and towns gathering information and watching for evil's poisonous influence, we often have to alter our appearance, and we sometimes need to change quickly.

"Remember also," Maelona continued, "that seers do not sleep as often as shifters. Working with my hands also helps me feel calm and focused while everyone else sleeps, and this is the result."

Blaez knew she was trying to downplay the significance of the work and thought she had put into this gift for the sake of remaining humble, so he let it go, simply stating, "Well, I thank you for your kind and thoughtful gift. It is truly appreciated." Then he leaned down to kiss her cheek.

That evening, Maelona and Blaez, in wolf form, dined with Gareth and Ailla in a farewell dinner. They spent the first part of the evening strategizing and reviewing their plans. But, as the evening went on, the topic changed, and they reminisced over amusing anecdotes from the past. Maelona had begun to feel more trusting and friendly toward Gareth, occasionally seeing similarities to his father. However, she still felt he had a little growing to do before his judgment could be trusted completely.

Gareth stood up and stretched. "Well," he said, "It is getting late, and I have a lot to do in the morning. So, I will see you all tomorrow."

"It is time for me to turn in as well," Maelona said. She stood to leave, and Blaez, as Wolf, stood with her. Before she and Wolf could leave for the evening, however, Ailla called to Blaez.

"Wolf, here!"

Maelona looked curiously at her mother. "I have a little treat for him," Ailla explained. Wolf padded over to her slowly, and when he reached her, she bent down with her hand outstretched, holding a morsel of meat for him. As he took it and chewed on it, Ailla bent down, pretending to stroke the fur behind his ear, and she whispered, "Meet me back here once the others are settled in for the night."

Once Gareth was asleep his room in the sorceress' sanctuary, and Maelona was back at her hut, Blaez returned, in human form, to speak with the sorceress.

"You wanted to see me, Sorceress"? he said.

"Yes," Ailla replied. "I would like to speak with you, but not here. Follow me."

Blaez followed Ailla through the twists and turns of the tunnels that made up her sanctuary. They had been walking for some time when she led him to a passageway near the back of the sanctuary, far underneath the escarpment. When they stopped, Ailla pressed her hand against the wall, and Blaez watched as her hand, and the section she was touching, lit with a blue light until a door appeared. Pushing against it, Ailla opened the door and motioned him inside.

Blaez had worked with the sorceress long enough to not be surprised by what had just occurred.

"I'm guessing that what you would like to discuss with me is of some importance if you are taking me here to talk," he commented.

"Yes," Ailla said. "But let's take a seat before we start."

Once they were seated comfortably inside with a small fire to warm them, the sorceress finally turned to address Blaez.

"My dear Blaez," she began, "I am sure you have figured out by now that, over the years, I have been preparing you to partner with my daughter through the dark times that are now upon us. Of course, at first, I didn't yet know the exact nature of what was coming. No one did. Now I would like to explain to you why, and tell you why I have chosen you.

"Maelona knows and understands the importance of her mission. There are still any number of uncertainties, but one thing we know is that her success or failure will determine the future of our realm. She is so young in shifter and seer years, and even more so in the years of a sorceress, yet so much rests upon her shoulders."

Ailla paused for a moment, her expression solemn and a little sad. She took a deep breath before continuing. "My daughter is special, Blaez. She is a seer, a shifter, and a sorcerer, born of two magical creatures who were both powerful in their own rights. I believe she has taken the best traits from each of us, although that may just be the pride of a mother." She smiled and glanced up at Blaez.

"Though she has the best parts of her father and me, she is unique. Years ago, I explained to you that we sorcerers harness energy and magic, draw it into ourselves from the natural world around us, and then refocus it where we need it." She looked up to Blaez again and caught his gaze in her intense expression.

"Maelona does not harness magic, Blaez," she continued emphatically. "Maelona *is* magic. It is a part of her just as surely as her heart and her head are. She is made up of cells and molecules that radiate and produce their own magic."

It took a moment for Blaez to make sense of Ailla's words. When he finally comprehended, he gave a start, and his eyes widened in surprise. Before he could respond, however, the sorceress continued.

"I may not be a seer, but I am a sorceress who has been around for a very long time. I am also Lona's mother," Ailla continued. "I carried her in my body. I could sense her magic. I can sense it still. I do not know if you are aware, Blaez, but Maelona has allowed me to work with her as she practices her magical skills. She only agrees to work with me when most others are sleeping. Even then, she insists on going some distance away, still fearing she may inadvertently hurt someone."

Blaez nodded. He had been around Maelona enough to know how important it was to her to not put anyone else at risk.

"When I work with her, Blaez," Ailla continued with feeling, "I can see her magic radiating out from her like an aura, touching the trees, the earth, the animals…anything that is close to her. I can feel her carefully contained and controlled power, and when we practice together, I can see and feel the tendrils of her magic coiling back inside of her as she focuses on having it do her bidding."

The sorceress paused for a moment.

"You may not know this Blaez," Ailla continued, "but this type of magic is extremely rare. Scota was the only other sorcerer I've heard of whose power emanated from within, and that was a millennium ago, according to our histories.

"What this means, Blaez, is that Maelona's magical abilities are limited only by her own mind and imagination. Her magic is very powerful, but it cannot be used to its full potential until she learns to forgive herself – to trust in herself and her power again. She must accept the magic as part of herself.

"Your job, dear Blaez, is to support her, to encourage her, to be her strength when her own wavers, throughout her physical and emotional journeys to come.

"When I first saw you at my door all those years ago, I knew it was fated. You were both indirectly linked by a common history. A very tragic history, yes, but it has affected both of you in similar ways. You are both trying to heal from tragic circumstances that neither of you had any say in or control over.

"You, more than anyone else, can help her to let go of the past and accept herself as she is, magic and all. When she releases some control of her emotions, she will relinquish some control over her magic as well. She will only reach her full potential, Blaez, when she lets her magic flow naturally."

"Why do you think I would be the best one to help her?" Blaez asked. "Yes, we are linked, but not in a happy or positive way. It was my own father who hurt her. It was my father who was responsible for her losing hers."

"See, this is why you are perhaps the only one who can truly help her." Ailla said. "You have both allowed yourselves to be molded by the same events. You have both been carrying guilt that was never really yours to bear." In a softer tone, she added, "You both, deep down inside, do not feel you are deserving of others' esteem, or of anyone's love."

She paused a moment, during which he allowed her words to sink into him. He wanted to be angry at what she was saying. He wanted to be able to deny it. However, he could not, because he realized it was the truth.

When Ailla spoke again, she said, "Because of your shared experiences, your shared understanding, you can heal each other."

Ailla took a deep breath and released it slowly, and Blaez knew she was coming to the end of her discourse. He continued to listen intently.

"I am not telling you this, Blaez, to put more pressure on you. I am telling you so I can ask you, as a mother and as a guardian of the realm, to please be patient with her and remain supportive through the trials to come. Do not give up on her. I know you care for her, so it should not be too much of a difficulty for you to give her what she needs to become her full and true self."

After a brief pause, Blaez responded with conviction. "You are our pack's sorceress, and my dear friend," he said. "I will always be grateful for your wisdom and insight. In this case, however, you need ask nothing of me. Your daughter already has my devotion, and it will not waver."

Ailla's smile spread across her face as Blaez spoke, and with his answer came an intuitive belief on her part that all would work out in the end.

"Go now, Blaez," Ailla told him. "You have a long journey ahead of you that begins in the morning."

As Blaez turned to leave, he hesitated for a moment, turning back to Ailla and taking her hand. "I do not know how long it will be before we see each other again. I will miss you, my friend."

"And I you," Ailla replied, before giving him the customary wolf shifter farewell and prayer for those embarking upon long journeys.

"May the moon shine luck and protection down upon you until fate crosses our paths again."

Chapter 12

Early the next morning, Maelona and Wolf made their way to the sorceress' sanctuary for the last time. Gareth was already sitting outside by the fire circle awaiting their arrival. Wolf stayed outside with Gareth as Maelona went inside to speak with her mother.

"I am glad you came to see me before beginning your journey, my daughter," Ailla said as Maelona entered the hearth room. "Sit and speak with me a little before you leave."

As Maelona sat across from her mother, Ailla handed her a cup of tea. Maelona did not fail to notice that the tea had already been prepared for her.

"Are you sure you don't have some seer in you too, Mother?" Maelona asked.

Ailla laughed. "Maybe I keep tea ready at all times, so it just looks like I know when someone's coming. But really, I didn't think you would leave without saying goodbye on your way through.

"How are you feeling this morning, my dear?" Ailla asked her daughter.

"To be honest," Maelona replied, "I am feeling…uncertain. In many ways, I feel unprepared to take on this task that has been placed upon me. However, the danger is upon us, and there is no more time to prepare."

After a pause, she continued, "You and the other elders and sorcerers expect me to finally put an end to this danger that

looms over us. Yet I know I am still young, and I am not as practiced in my magic as I should be." Looking into her mother's
eyes, her worry evident in her own, she voiced her fears: "What
if I cannot complete the task you have set out for me? What if I
am not strong enough?"

Ailla knew these fears of her own shortcomings were not
something that Maelona would share with just anyone, and the
mother in her was glad that her Lona was comfortable sharing
with her. She had feared that their years of estrangement would
hold her daughter back from opening up to her now. However,
this was clearly not the case, and she was glad for it.

Ailla took a deep breath and let it out again before addressing her daughter's concerns.

"Over the years," she began, "I have questioned our decision many times. Sometimes, I feel certain that your father and I
made the right choice for the future of the realm. At other times,
I regret that I have placed such a burden on an innocent who
wasn't given any choice—my own daughter at that. Yet I have
never doubted that you would be able to handle the path that
has been set before you."

Ailla leaned toward Maelona and grasped her hand, "You
are strong, Lona. *So* strong! And you are good to your very core.
I have known this about you since you were just a small child,
gently correcting the other children when they would steal
another's toy or were cruel to one another. But you must come
to accept, my beloved daughter, that you are never alone. You
have people in your life who care for you and who would like
nothing more than to support you in any way they can. You just
have to let them.

"You cannot continue to hold people at arm's length,
Maelona. You need to let them in. You must let go of your fear
that you may hurt those you let close to you. You have to stop
blaming yourself."

"But it was my fault," Maelona interjected.

"No, my dear. It was an accident. If there was anyone at
fault, it would be your father and me," Ailla responded sadly. "In
our desire to keep you protected, to keep your existence hidden

for as long as possible, we sheltered you from the outside world. You had never even glimpsed the darker side of life until it was upon you. You were completely unprepared, and, as your parents, it was our job to prepare you. It was a job that we failed at."

Seeing the sadness and guilt in her mother's eyes, Maelona had a sudden realization. She squeezed her mother's hand. "Maybe we're both wrong," she said. "Maybe we're both placing the blame where it doesn't belong. After all, it was Blyth Murdax who made the choice to act as he did."

They stayed like that, contemplating their words and holding on to one another for a few moments before Ailla stood up, saying, "Now go! I will see you again at the Great Gate."

While Maelona was inside with her mother saying her goodbyes, Gareth sat waiting on a rock next to the now unlit fire circle. Suddenly feeling the hair on the back of his neck stand up, he looked to his left, only to find Wolf staring at him unblinkingly.

The gaze from those icy blue eyes seemed to bore a hole into him, and he shivered. He tried to distract himself by double-checking his pack, which sat at his feet. Once he was satisfied he hadn't forgotten anything he looked up again, only to find Wolf staring at him still.

He looked forward again as he heard Maelona approach. "Finally!" he said. "Your wolf is giving me the shivers. Why does he stare at me so intently? Does he stare at everyone like that?"

Maelona walked past Gareth toward Wolf with her hand outstretched, and he rose and padded over to meet her. "Animals can be peculiar like that," she replied with a smirk as she stroked the fur on the animal's head. Turning to face Gareth again, she continued, "He is just trying to figure you out; to get a feel for who you are. The novelty will wear off once he gets to know you."

"He is quite a large wolf. I have never seen one as large. Is he a particular sub-species of wolf that grows to a greater size than most?"

"Maybe," Maelona answered. "Though it is difficult to say for certain. He just started following me one day," she said, her mouth quirking up at the corner. She scratched the top of Wolf's head, adding affectionately, "However, he has become invaluable to me since then."

"Is that a pack he is carrying?" Gareth asked curiously. "It looks much like your own."

"Yes," Maelona answered while still grinning. "Like I said, he is invaluable. Carrying things is just one of his many uses."

They started out on the north path that went up and around the sorceress' sanctuary. As they began walking, Gareth responded to Maelona's comment.

"Yes, I can see how having such a beast would be useful for a female such as yourself, who travels alone." Still looking forward, Maelona raised her brows and shook her head slightly, but otherwise did not respond.

"We have not had the opportunity to really converse or get to know one another during my stay here, what with the meetings and preparations, and me being confined to bed while I healed," Gareth continued. "It's too bad, really. I could have used some company." He flashed Maelona his most charming smile.

"I am sure the sorceress provided good company," Maelona replied. "Many travel long distances just to have the opportunity to speak with her. She is very well-respected for her wisdom and insight."

"Oh, without doubt," Gareth agreed. "I did enjoy my conversations with her. During my short stay, she has given me much to think about. Like you, however, she was often drawn away on business."

"I am not a very social being, anyway. I usually prefer to be on my own," Maelona said. "I probably would have bored you with my lack of social skills. And aside from that," she added, "you came to us for help, and help we shall provide. While your injuries have kept us from returning to your father as soon as you would have liked, the time you have taken to heal has given us the advantage of being able to better prepare…and not just for your father and Eastgate, but for what may follow as well."

"I truly appreciate what you are doing for my father and our kingdom. I just hope we get there before it's too late to stop whatever evil has crept in." Gareth immediately realized how that sounded, so he added, "I don't want to sound ungrateful at all. That was not my intention. I simply wanted to say that I'm looking forward to the opportunity to get to know you better during our travels." As he leaned his head forward and to the side to try to catch Maelona's gaze, he heard a low growl coming from Maelona's right. Yet, she did not seem to react to either his or Wolf's actions.

"Yes, I am sure our journey will be quite educational for you," Maelona replied. "I hope you take the lessons to heart."

They walked on in silence for some time before Gareth asked a question that had been scratching at the back of his mind. "You say this dark sorcerer wants to subjugate the realm, and everyone at the meeting seemed shocked that demonkin followed me into the forest. Then there are the attacks on Eastgate. Do you think this sorcerer has already begun his plans for taking over the realm?"

"Oh, I'm sure he has," Maelona replied. "The real worry is that the demonkin have made it this far, into the Sacred Forest no less, and we hadn't foreseen it. I am going to have to try harder."

"I thought you said you don't get to choose the visions you get?"

"Not normally, no. However, I have a few advantages that the others do not. I just usually chose not to use them."

Gareth got the impression, by her expression as she spoke, that whatever she intended to do was particularly distasteful to her.

"I don't suppose you'd care to share what you mean, would you?"

"No, I wouldn't," she replied. "At least, not yet."

They walked on in this manner for the rest of the day. Gareth tried to impress Maelona with his charm and conversational skills to get her to open up some. However, she remained impassive. But he did count one small victory for himself: by the time the sun had started to lower itself onto the horizon hours later, Wolf had stopped growling at him regularly.

Maelona headed off the path and walked into the forest.

Gareth and Wolf followed.

"Is it wise to wander off the path?" Gareth inquired.

"It's wiser than setting up camp in the middle of the path," Maelona responded.

When she reached a small clearing in the trees, she turned in a circle to take in her surroundings. The area was perfect for providing shelter. The overhanging branches opened to a clear view of the sky in the center.

"We will camp here for the night," Maelona stated.

"Good," Gareth replied. "I'm famished. I hope we will be having something other than the berries and unleavened bread we've been eating all day. Did you manage to pack some meat during your preparations?" he asked.

"I did," Maelona answered, "but that is for when other food sources run scarce."

"Well, that's a disappointment. I was looking forward to something substantial."

Maelona looked at Gareth and spoke with the slightest touch of exasperation, but also humor, in her voice. "You really are not much of a woodsman, are you, Prince?"

"Well, to be honest," he responded, unable to hide his grin, "I am the Prince of Eastgate. When I was a child, there were often threats to the royal family and, in particular, to the heir. So, my mother kept me fairly sheltered, and I rarely left the city walls. My father tried to fight her on this, saying the future king should be prepared for anything. My mother, however, liked to dote, and she could be quite spirited when crossed. So, her will won out most of the time." He chuckled at this. "She passed away when I was 15, so my father got a little tougher with me then."

"I am sorry for your loss," Maelona replied simply, not wanting to make him uncomfortable by prying.

Gareth nodded his thanks to her, then continued. "I received some training of course: sword fighting, archery, knife throwing, hand to hand combat, basic survival skills. I practice fighting skills regularly, but I haven't had much opportunity to practice survival skills."

"Has your father never taken you out hunting?"

Maelona asked.

"Well yes, but as I said, there were always threats, so we were always surrounded by our men…men who seemed to want to stay on our good side by doing much of the work for me."

It was on the tip of Maelona's tongue to ask Gareth why his father had sent him on this mission instead of someone else, but she held back her curiosity. She was quite sure she already knew the answer to that question, and that she was providing an instructional service that the king wished his son to receive.

"You will get your meat, Prince, do not fear," she said instead. "Lesson number one in basic survival - which I have been trying to demonstrate to you all day – is, inside the forest, nature shall provide." She lifted her hands to gesture around her. "I have been showing you this by teaching you which berries are safe to eat and how to find edible roots. Now, search around the area for dead wood for the fire, and I will go forage for our supper." Wolf stood and followed her as she headed into the trees.

An hour later, Gareth had a good pile of branches and dead wood which he was carefully stacking in a small fire pit he had fashioned from stones. He was determined to show Maelona that he was not completely inept and could be a useful companion.

He had to admit to himself, however, that he liked poking at her by pretending to be even less skilled and more spoiled than he actually was. He was sure, of course, that her experiences had made her much more skilled and knowledgeable than himself, but still, he was not completely useless. So, he placed some wood in the fire pit, being careful to leave space for the air to flow through, and carefully arranged tinder underneath.

He had just started the fire with the flint and steel he always carried in his pack when he heard movement behind him, and he turned to find Maelona walking toward the fire carrying a large bird of some kind.

"I see you've had a successful hunt."

"I have indeed," Maelona replied.

"Is that a flightless bird?" Gareth asked.

"It is not," she replied.

"But you're not carrying a bow and arrow," he observed.

"No, I am not," she replied. "However, I do have these," she said. She took a throwing knife out of her chest strap and spun it in her hand before returning it to its place.

"Hmm," he replied with an arched brow, as he watched Maelona set the large bird down on a large rock a few feet from the campfire.

She turned to him and said, "Now you will learn how to clean and prepare a meal that has been freshly caught."

"This is exactly the kind of thing someone would do *for* me back at Eastgate," Gareth responded, lips pressed together in mock disgust.

"And it is exactly the kind of thing you need to be prepared to do for yourself," Maelona said. "You are the future King and Guardian of Eastgate. You may not always have a party of men with you, and you need to learn how to rely on yourself if need be."

"I can rely on myself just fine," Gareth said in a fake irritated tone. Then he jumped as he heard a loud snort from behind him. Turning around, he noticed Wolf sitting just this side of the tree line. "By father's beard!" Gareth exclaimed. "Has he been here this whole time?"

Maelona couldn't help it; she burst out laughing. She noticed Wolf looking as if he were rolling his eyes and shaking his head over by the side of the clearing, and it made her laugh even more.

She had been aware that Gareth had been exaggerating the ineptness, playing up the part of spoiled prince most likely in an attempt to lighten the tension between them. There was no way her old friend Niall would leave his heir untrained and unprepared, however. There was too much at stake. She was as sure of that as she was that Gareth lacked real-world experience.

She was also sure, of course, that he was still a spoiled prince to some degree, but she at least had to admire him for playing up his own weaknesses to try to make her feel more comfortable and confident around him.

Maelona had known before leaving the village that she would not give in to Gareth's attempts to charm her, at least not in the way he seemed to hope. After all, he was barely more than a child in many ways, and the son of an old friend. She had to admit, however, that he was, indeed, a bit of a charmer. For example, she had not expected him to use this self-deprecating humor. Unexpectedly, she had been quite amused, and then Wolf's reaction had tipped her over the edge.

"Alright then, Prince, show me what you can do to make this catch edible," Maelona said to Gareth, so he set about cleaning and preparing the bird for the fire. Meanwhile, Maelona set a flat stone over the fire and set about slicing some of the roots and tubers they had dug up earlier in the day. She then set these on the hot stone to cook. Every once in a while, she would check Gareth's progress and give him some pointers.

"Isn't this nice?" Gareth mused at one point.

"What?" Maelona asked.

"Just you and I, preparing a meal together. Such an image of domestic happiness and comfort." He let out a dramatic, happy sigh. "Doesn't it stir longings in you, as it does for me?"

"Well, first of all, you live in a castle, so I don't imagine this is the kind of domestic happiness you are used to seeing. Don't you have cooks and servants?"

"I have friends in town. I see things."

"Second of all, it isn't just you and I," she said, gesturing to Wolf with the knife in her hand. As if to back her up, Wolf padded over and sat at her side.

"I don't think pets can really be considered chaperones," Gareth muttered.

"And lastly, you are a baby when one considers the number of years I have behind me compared to you."

"What do you mean? You look younger than I do, and the others at the fire circle kept mentioning how young you are. You can't be older than me, and if you are, it can't be by much."

"Let's just say, I first met your father when he was a child."

Gareth considered that for a moment. Then, his eyes widened.

"What?" he said. "How is that possible?"

"That's a story for another time. For now, focus on cooking the fowl before it burns."

A little later, when they had mostly finished their meal, Maelona sat leaning against Wolf, feeding him bits of what was left of the meat. "Shouldn't we be saving that for our next meal?" Gareth asked.

"Don't worry, I have already put some inside a pouch along with some herbs that will keep it fresh a little longer than normal. If we happen upon some more of these herbs during our travels, I will point them out to you. They can be invaluable on long journeys."

Gareth stretched and yawned, saying, "Well, it's late, and we still have much traveling ahead of us in the morning. I think I shall get some rest now." Then he grinned and looked at Maelona. "There is a chill in the air tonight. Perhaps we should consider sharing body warmth."

"You needn't worry about me," Maelona replied, leaning into Wolf. "I have my own fur blanket. But you could perhaps lay on the other side of Wolf. I'm sure he wouldn't mind."

Gareth looked at Wolf, who emitted a low, rumbling growl as he met his eyes. "I think I'll pass," he said. "Come to think of it, I do have a cloak in my pack that should do just fine," he said with amusement. Maelona shook her head and could not help but give a little smile in return.

A couple of hours later, while Gareth slept soundly, Maelona gave a little tug on Wolf's fur and stood up to walk silently into the forest. Wolf followed her until they ended up at the top of a little grassy hill, where she sat and looked up at the night sky.

Lingering behind so he could shift, Blaez shrugged off his pack and dressed in his pants before coming to sit beside Maelona. He loved this new pack that Maelona had made for him. It was so very convenient to be able to carry his things with him, no matter what form he was in.

Maelona turned to look at him, giving him a small smile before gazing up at the stars again.

"Tell me, my Lona," Blaez said. "What is on your mind?"

"I was just thinking about what forms a person's true nature. How much our parentage forms who we are as opposed to our experiences. And then, how much fate influences our paths as opposed to our own desires.

"For instance," she continued, "Gareth shares his father's hair and eye color and even mirrors his easy charm to some degree. Yet his father was already more worldly and intuitive when I first met him many years ago, and he was much younger than Gareth then, by human standards.

"Then there is you," she said. "I was truly surprised when my mother told me who your father was, though I had already spent some time with you by then. I am not surprised very often."

She looked at him and smiled again. "You are a wonder to me, Blaez. I could see nothing but good in your eyes when we met; I could see your desire to help and protect. Never once have I thought that you deserved to do your father's penance, yet you happily take it upon yourself to ease as much of the pain he left behind as possible."

Reaching across to take Maelona's hand in his, Blaez responded, "Well, when it comes to one's nature, I believe each of the elements you mentioned have a part to play. More than that, however, I believe it is the choices we make that have the final say, as you yourself once said. We can choose to be happy, to lead a good life. We can decide on the kind of person we want to be, and then make a thousand small choices each day to keep us on our path.

"I was lucky I had my mother," Blaez said after a short pause. "She was calm and considerate, patient and kind. When I was young, I used to think she was weak for putting up with my father and his violent ways. Over time, however, I've come to realize that she had her own kind of quiet strength. She never gave up or cowered to my father. She showed me that there is always a better way; that there is always a choice."

Looking up to meet Blaez's affectionate gaze, Maelona said softly, "You are very lucky to have had such a positive influence in your life. Not every young one is so lucky. I wish I could have met her."

Blaez smiled at Maelona and said, "From having spent years with your mother, I would venture to say you are one of the lucky ones yourself. I have seen her love and devotion to you, and even in your absence she is always thinking of you and speaking of you."

Maelona's smile brightened her face as she responded, "I was lucky to have both of my parents." She spoke slowly and thoughtfully when she continued. "You know, there was a brief period of time when I doubted my parents' love for me." Blaez raised his eyebrows in surprise at this, but Maelona continued without acknowledging his reaction.

"Back when I first discovered that I had been conceived with a purpose, I questioned whether they truly loved me or if I was just a tool, a means to an end, for them. But they have proven their love for me time and again over the years, with my father even giving the ultimate sacrifice to protect me from harm. And now, as you may have noticed at the meeting with the elders, my mother has shown her reluctance at allowing me to continue on the very path I was born for."

Blaez knew that the sorceress believed Maelona was the only one who could carry and wield the Ternias. However, he did not know how or why, or what the ultimate goal or task was. Now he found himself wondering about the nature of her task and the amount of danger involved. Therefore, he couldn't help but ask, "So, what exactly is this path you were born for?"

Maelona placed her hand softly on his cheek and answered solemnly. "I will tell you when the time is right, mo grá. However, this is not that time."

Blaez figured he should be feeling disappointed at the lack of an answer, yet he was distracted by the feeling of warmth and contentment spreading through him at her touch. He absorbed the term of endearment she had used for him. It meant *my love*.

"As for choices," Maelona went on, locking his gaze once again, "I feel you and I were meant for one another. Yet I also can't help but feel as though making the choice for us to be together would be selfish of me. Dangerous times are upon us, and my personal mission is a particularly perilous one."

"You may be a seer," Blaez said, giving her an affectionate smile, "but you have said that things can always change. We may never truly know what the future will bring until it is our present. So, I choose to live for what I know to be right at this moment. I choose to be yours."

With those words, Blaez leaned forward and pressed his lips to hers in a soft kiss that quickly turned passionate.

Later, Maelona would look back at this moment and marvel at the fact that, though her emotions were high and she could feel her power traveling like electricity through herself and Blaez, this time it felt natural and instinctual. This time, she did not lose control or pull away.

Chapter 13

In the next few days following their shared moment, Blaez noticed Maelona had pulled back somewhat. She had not mentioned their kiss since, though Blaez found his mind drawn back to that moment time and again. He had been prepared to be patient before, and now, since their talk, he understood her reservations all the better. He had no doubt in his mind about Maelona's feelings, or about the connection they undoubtedly shared. However, she had much resting on her shoulders, and her worries were not unfounded. He was willing to wait until she was ready to reach out to him and to allow herself to rely on him.

Blaez also noticed that the closer they traveled toward Eastgate, the quieter and more thoughtful Maelona became. Given she was a seer, he knew this likely meant there was trouble ahead.

In the time Blaez had traveled with her, each morning Maelona had climbed to the top of the highest tree to scout things out. Now she had taken to doing the same at dusk and again a couple of hours after nightfall.

On this particular night, after she climbed down from the tree, she sat on a rock at the edge of their camp with a serious countenance. Calling Wolf over to her, she pressed her forehead to his furry one. Speaking in a low voice, she said, "It's time."

Always one to try to diffuse tense situations, Gareth asked,

"Time for what? You aren't going to allow him to make a meal of me now, are you?"

Ignoring his attempt at humor, Maelona looked Gareth in the eye as she spoke. "There are things within your city and within our forest that you would normally not be privy to, Gareth, until you were officially sworn in as King of Eastgate. Given the current situation in the realm, however, there are things you need to know now. But before I tell you, I ask you to remember that, at the moment, we have the element of surprise on our side. We need to keep it. Always remember that not everyone is what or who they seem."

This warning made Gareth think about the situation with his father and who could have gotten that close to him, and how. Before he had time to dwell on this concept in any detail, however, Maelona continued. Keeping her eyes on Gareth, she simply said, "Blaez."

Gareth looked at her in confusion for just a moment before movement to Maelona's left caught his attention. Wolf had gotten to his feet and Gareth looked on in astonishment as the great, black beast started to shimmer, expand and re-form before him. It began to stand on its hind legs until it was upright and, even more surprising, human, in front of him. *Well, not really human*, he mused. *Definitely shifter.*

The man lifted his head as he stood to his full height, and Gareth found himself looking at the same ice blue eyes that had stared at him so often, making him feel almost paranoid, over the past couple of weeks. The male before him was tall, broad, and well-muscled - more so than any of the males at the castle.

Now that he knew that Wolf, or Blaez rather, was a shifter, he could see the differences between a man and a shifter in human form. He was, in fact, much larger than any of the guards at the castle, both in height and musculature. He had an intensity about him that was intimidating. Yet he also realized that Blaez could still pass as a very large human male if one were not expecting a shifter.

"Well then," Gareth began hesitantly. "This explains a whole lot." With a mischievous grin in Maelona's direction, he added,

"Now I understand why you've been so unaffected by my charms."

"Yes," Blaez retorted in a deep, rumbling voice. "I am sure it has nothing to do with how annoying and arrogant you are."

"Ouch!" Gareth quipped, mock-flinching. "Who would have ever expected such sharp sarcasm from a male who sounds like he is growling when he speaks?" Then he added, "The eyes still give me the shivers, by the way. Would you please be so kind as to point those things elsewhere?"

"The females do not seem to mind them," Blaez responded. "Usually, they want a closer look."

Maelona chuckled and shook her head. "You two can duel to prove who is the manliest once the war is over. Right now, though, I need you both focused."

Blaez tightened the straps of his pack, which dangled loosely after his shift, so they were the proper size for his human form. He removed the pack from his back, reached inside for his pants, and quickly put them on.

Blaez took a seat on a rock next to where Maelona sat, so close to her that they were touching arm to arm. Then he narrowed his eyes at Gareth across the almost-dead embers of their earlier fire. They always extinguished their campfires before the night took over so as not to be spotted by any who roamed too close or who may be keeping watch.

Before Gareth could respond to Blaez's actions, however, Maelona began to speak.

"Have you ever been outside of the Sacred Forest, Blaez?" she asked.

"Yes, but only on a couple of occasions to outlying villages," he answered.

"Well, be prepared for a completely different way of life," she warned.

Looking to Gareth, she went on. "Are you surprised that Blaez is a shifter, Gareth? That Blaez and Wolf are one and the same?"

"Well, to be honest, yes," Gareth answered. "I have never seen a shifter before today. I had assumed that their species had either died out or was on its way out."

"That is not by accident," Maelona said. "When the seer

people were almost wiped out about three hundred years ago, we were hunted by those who feared our abilities, such as humans, shifters, and other magical beings. The evil that had crept in behind the scenes made sure to plant the belief that we were almost omniscient and played with people's lives. But this is far from the case.

"As I mentioned before, it is extremely rare that any seer can choose what they see, and at what point in time. When we have our dream-visions, they seem to be random and usually point us to where danger lies. It is like the universe itself sends us where we are most needed.

"However, the idea that we could see anything about anyone, then change our appearance to sneak in unobserved and manipulate lives, was a very frightening idea to most, and these rumors spread like wildfire. We were hunted down in cold blood, with most seers refusing to fight those who were being manipulated by an evil hand. Many seers died, and some others were captured by those who wished to use us against their enemies. The rest went into hiding, here in the sacred forest.

"When the dust settled, however, many humans and other non-magical beings now looked to the shifters (and those who held magical powers of any sort) with paranoia and suspicion, even though humans far outnumbered the rest. In the end, ironically, many of the magical races ended up here with us in the Foraoise Naofa." Maelona chuckled humorlessly, then added, "Lucky for them, the seers knew and understood what had happened, and did not blame them."

"If there are so many magical beings here, so close to human habitation, why are there not more sightings? Why don't we know more about you?" Gareth asked.

"Those are very good questions," Maelona replied. "And they are tied to the reason why the battle is headed our way. Do you remember what the sorceress said about the magical ley lines, and the magical energy they contain?"

"I do," Gareth replied.

"Well, where better for a large group of magical beings to hide but within a great source of magical power? The Sorcerers of the Light at that time used the power of the ley lines to create magical defenses around the forest, thereby effectively shielding us from the outside world. Of course, other beings do travel here from time to time, such as yourself. Tell me, Gareth, how did you feel when you entered the forest?"

Gareth paused in thought for a moment before answering, "Well, I felt a little uneasy. I might have turned around again if my father had not tasked me with venturing here to find Maddock Sima."

"That sense of dread," Maelona stated, "turns to a belief that unimaginable horrors await you, and the more darkness a being holds inside of them, the stronger the feeling gets. The uneasiness you felt is to be expected. Everyone holds at least a little darkness inside, after all. What is surprising is that the demonkin who pursued you were not paralyzed with fear. I can only guess that they carried something that could neutralize that part of the magical protection, which is something else to be concerned about.

"As for why there hasn't been more sightings," she continued, "there have been many more than you would suspect. How would you know, for example, if a traveler passing through your town was truly human or not?"

After thinking about this for a moment, Gareth answered, "Well, now that you ask, I suppose I would not know."

"Do you know," Maelona continued, "that every person around our fire circle the night before we left, every last one aside from yourself, was a shifter?"

Gareth's eyes opened wide in disbelief. But then, after a moment, he shook his head and said, "I guess I shouldn't really be surprised about that after the information you just gave me."

"The reason I am telling you all of this," Maelona said, "is that in about a day and a half we will be leaving the protection of the Sacred Forest. And once we pass the treeline, you need to be prepared for anything. Demonkin can generally be easy to spot, of course, being physically very different than us. But there are some demonkin who can hide their appearance."

"Like the seers and shifters," Gareth observed.

"Well, yes and no," Maelona responded. "Yes, we can all change our appearance to some degree, but with shifters and seers, it is as much physical as magical. Shifters' bodies really do change from man to animal and back again. Seers physically manipulate factors present in our bodies to change our outward appearance, like hair and eye color, so we really, physically change as well. With the demonkin," she continued, "it's all an illusion. If you get close enough to touch one, for example, it is possible to notice that what you feel may not be the same as what you see. Demonkin can make themselves look like anyone, so if you have doubts about a person, you can use this as a test."

"Well, all of this information certainly answers a number of questions I was left with after the meeting. So, I have to ask, why are you explaining this now?" Gareth said. "Why didn't you explain it all at the meeting?"

"Everyone else at the circle already had this information," Blaez said.

"Yes," Maelona agreed. "Plus," she added, "you did not need to know this information then, but you do now."

"And why is that?" Gareth asked with a cautious tone.

"As I watched from the trees," Maelona answered, "I could see firelight just outside the forest. This could be campfires of those sent to watch the forest. After all, I am certain that you did not disappear into the forest, with three demonkin disappearing behind you, without being noticed."

"Well, this is great news," Gareth said sarcastically.

"I am afraid it's not the worst," Maelona replied.

Blaez looked at her in concern. "What is it, mo grá?" he asked.

Looking at him, she responded, "There were fires further on, as well. Into the farmsteads. I fear they are invading the farmland and building their numbers before attacking the city."

"What do we do?" Gareth asked.

"Well, for now, I suggest we get some rest. We will need our strength," Maelona responded. Then she turned to look Blaez in the eye once again. "I will need to sleep tonight," she said meaningfully, and Blaez nodded in understanding.

Maelona sat looking out at the myriad of colors dancing above the treetops as the sun began to rise the next morning. She had started a small fire to cook a simple breakfast of leftover fowl and roots for herself, Blaez, and Gareth. The sky was just light enough that the fire would not be visible from a distance. The men had not stirred yet, and she used the quiet stillness of the early morning to help focus her thoughts.

After she had sent out her message to the other seers the night before, Maelona had fallen asleep. As soon as she stopped guiding her own thoughts, visions began to flicker in, and she was now quietly contemplating what they meant.

At first, when she'd been in the state between purposely sending messages and falling asleep, a vision had flickered in from Edan in the west. She saw an arrow tinged with green. She knew this was a warning, something she had to look out for. Immediately following that, an image had flickered in from Talwyn in the south, showing battle. But it was not a battle at Southgate. She knew this because, in the vision, she saw Blaez under attack. This was something Talwyn had seen in a vision of her own. Another danger Maelona had to watch out for. She tried to shake off the details of the vision because, if she thought too much about it, she would not be able to focus on what needed to be done.

Once she had fallen fully asleep, Maelona began receiving visions of a figure in a dark cloak. His face was hidden inside the cloak's cowl. They were in a cavern of some sort, and she could hear eerie sounds of hissing and stone scraping over stone. She could also hear a name being whispered over and over. She had listened intently, trying to make it out, and just as she had started to get it, she awoke, and it was lost to her.

Maelona was certain that the dark figure from her dream was the sorcerer behind the quest to take over Sterrenvar and enslave the good people of the realm. No other seer or sorcerer of the time had been able to even glimpse this evil being before, and she wondered why she was seeing him now. Was he becoming weaker, perhaps overtaxing himself, or was she becoming stronger?

To be honest, she knew that each time she took a step closer to opening up to others and, in particular, to Blaez, she could feel her magic beginning to flow through her more freely. When she began to partially let go of her tight control on her emotions, she also let go of some of her control over her magic, hence allowing it to flow more naturally through her. Even her budding comradery with Gareth added to this feeling.

For the first time in a long time, she felt hopeful that she could free her emotions. She wanted to truly allow others in so she wouldn't have to feel alone in the world. On the opposite side of that, however, was the fear of the pain of loss that still lingered. Yet, she knew everyone had to face this fear at some time in their lives. Perhaps she was finally ready to take that chance.

Maybe she could finally have a meaningful relationship with a male she cared deeply for. As close as she was to Anwyl, she had never let him in the way she had with Blaez. There were parts of herself she had always kept guarded. She now felt hopeful that she would be ready when the time came to face her fears, and her foes. And she knew she would no longer be fighting her battles alone.

Maelona suddenly felt lighter, freer, as she realized that her self-acceptance would open many more options for dealing with what was to come. She now understood what she needed to do.

A rustling sound next to her indicated that Blaez was waking. Rousing himself, he moved over to where she sat. Then he reached his hand out and stroked his thumb along her cheek. "Good morning, mo grá," he said. "How was your sleep?"

"Oddly, both informative and confusing at the same time," Maelona replied with a small smile as she gazed up at him.

Maelona knew that Blaez was always interested in what she was thinking. She could see it written on his face now that he was tempted to ask for more details. However, she also knew he understood her well enough to know that she would share what they needed to know, if anything, once she had sorted it through herself. So, instead of questioning her, he said, "I am going to make my way back to the brook we passed to collect some water. I believe I'll also take a swim to refresh myself while I am there."

Maelona simply nodded to him with a smile before once again becoming engrossed in her thoughts.

A short time later, Gareth awoke as well. He made his way over to the fire, which was mostly embers by now, and partook of the small meal Maelona had prepared. "So where is your wolf?" Gareth asked.

"He went to the brook to collect water and wash up," she replied, not reacting to the slight he feigned by not using Blaez's name.

"Now that we are alone," Gareth said, "I would like to ask you about something that's been on my mind since I found out that Wolf is really Blaez."

"Go ahead," Maelona said with an encouraging nod.

"I have to ask you, Maelona - you are a seer, and Blaez is a shifter. My people are human. As far as my people know, your kind had gone the way of legend. And when you are spoken about, there is still an undercurrent of fear and superstition."

He paused and took a deep breath before continuing. "I observed the attitude from some of the others at the meeting once it became known that you are a seer, and that was from another magical race. Do you really believe all our peoples can work together?"

Evidently, Gareth held serious doubts. His flippant façade was stripped away for once, and Maelona could see apprehension in his face and body language. She could hear it in his voice. And she understood his reservations. So, she looked him in the eye as she answered. "I do not just believe it can happen, Gareth. I know it must happen."

From their dream-visions, she and the other seers knew there were a few possible scenarios, but she did not want to leave Gareth any room for doubt, so she kept this to herself.

"Not one of the many and varied races in the realm can take on the evil that threatens all of us by itself and hope to be victorious," she continued. "Not only are we facing this sorcerer of unknown magical abilities, but our visions have shown he has the support of the demonkin, the snowbeasts, and the human tribes that live in the northern mountain range. Now, with recent revelations, I fear he is bringing his followers into the conflict both sooner and further south than we anticipated. We will all need to stand together to resist being used as slaves and fodder for the evil beings who wish to subdue us.

"You and I, Gareth," she continued emphatically, "are leaders amongst our people. It is our responsibility, our duty, to bring our people together to protect the realm.

"It shouldn't prove too difficult," she added with a wry smile. "Nothing brings people together more readily than having to face a common enemy. And watching the three of us work together will provide an excellent example to our peoples."

The sun was high in the sky when Maelona, Blaez, and Gareth cautiously approached the edge of the forbidden forest. Maelona and Blaez had been watching for signs of anything passing here that did not belong. A couple of hours earlier they had come across the telltale freshly broken saplings and bushes and tracks too large to be human. However, they knew they weren't shifter either.

Maelona took a careful look, noting that while the footprints were similar to human, or shifter in human form, they were also broader and thicker at the heel.

"Demonkin," she stated.

They veered off the main path, staying hidden in the trees as best they could. They moved along the perimeter of the forest, a couple of meters in, moving toward where Maelona had seen the nearest fire two nights ago. This was the place where the neighboring farmland brushed up against the Sacred Forest.

Peering through the trees, Maelona and Blaez, with their shifter-heightened eyesight, were able to make out the burnt-out husk of a barn. A short way beyond that was the dwelling of those who farmed the land. From here it looked intact, but Maelona knew from her visions that the demonkin who had been hunting Gareth were still close by. Only three had pursued him into the forest, but there were others who had followed but stayed behind.

"I have a plan," Maelona said to the others. "There are demonkin inside that dwelling, and we need to draw them out. Since they were sent here to hunt down the Prince of Eastgate, I think Gareth should approach from the front, walking down the path as if he were returning from his trip and on his way home. Blaez and I will approach from the back, in wolf form, so we do not attract attention."

Blaez's eyebrows shot up in surprise at this suggestion, and a huge smile spread across his face.

As for Gareth, he looked confused for a moment before asking, "You mean Blaez will be in wolf form, right?"

"No," Maelona clarified. "I mean we will both be in wolf form."

"Wait, are you telling me that seers can shift too?" Gareth asked in surprise.

"Not usually, no," Maelona answered. "However, I am only half seer. My father was seer, but my mother, the sorceress, is a shifter."

"So, you are saying that you have the abilities of a seer *and* of a shifter?"

"Yes," was Maelona's simple response. "Though I have not shifted in over forty years."

"Over forty years!" Gareth exclaimed. "Just how old are you? You look like you can't have more than twenty-five years, at most! I really thought you were just trying to throw me off when you said you knew my father as a child."

"I am not nearly as old as the others you met at the sorceress' sanctuary, I assure you. I am, in fact, considered to be barely into adulthood by most in that group, as you recall."

Gareth puffed out a big breath before putting his hands on his hips and walking a small circle. "Okay, from now on, only tell me what I need to know. I do not need to be passing out in shock as we're about to take on a bunch of demonkin."

Maelona could not help but chuckle at Gareth's antics. While she knew he must be surprised by what he had just learned, she also knew he liked to exaggerate as a form of humor.

"Gareth, you walk back to the path in the forest, then follow it out toward the dwelling. Blaez and I will shift and approach from the back. Since they are not looking out for animals but are rather watching for you, we should be able to go unnoticed. Once you draw them out, we will check out the area for any other demonkin so we will not be taken by surprise before heading to join you. We will also need to check for any survivors, but let us neutralize the danger first."

A little more subdued than before, Gareth nodded to Maelona before turning and heading back the way they had come.

"Gareth!" Maelona called before he was out of earshot. He paused and turned to look at her. "In case we get tied up, do you think you can handle a demonkin or two on your own?"

"Of course I can! I am the Prince of Eastgate after all," he called back with a smile.

Maelona thought back to the way he had fought the first time she had ever laid eyes on him. Knowing he was still feeling the effects from the last attack, though he was mostly healed, she felt concerned for him.

"Don't plant your feet," she advised. "Keep moving. Demonkin are not agile. Use that to your benefit."

Gareth's smile softened at the concern in her voice. He nodded to her once again before turning and continuing on his way.

Maelona then turned her attention back to Blaez. "It has been a very long time since I have shifted, Blaez, and I have never tried to hide my true coloring in wolf form. This may take me a moment," she said. She then quickly undressed and placed her clothing in her pack. "My pack is expandable like yours, but I did not make it with shifting in mind. I hope it holds up," she commented as she secured it back into place and tugged on the clasps to loosen the straps.

Turning to face Blaez, Maelona looked into his eyes. He could tell she was nervous and unsure, and he held her gaze to help anchor and support her. Then she took a deep breath, and Blaez watched as her form shivered and expanded before him.

Blaez could not help but suck in a sharp breath. The brown eyes he had been gazing into were now the color of amethyst, very like her mother's, yet more vibrant and bright somehow. It was hard for him to break her gaze to take in her wolf form, but when he managed to do so, he was glad. Her fur was pure white at the base, tipped with a pale lavender color at the very ends. On all fours, her head came almost to his shoulder height. She was truly an impressive creature.

He raised his hands to stroke along her jaws, tilting her head up as he looked into her eyes once again. "Beautiful," he whispered. Then, in the same moment, he watched as her eyes morphed into a golden-green color. Letting go of her face and stepping back, he saw that she had changed her coloring to match a rather large, but otherwise normal-looking, gray wolf. With no further delay, Blaez quickly removed his own pack, took off his pants, and put them inside. He then donned his pack again, loosened the straps, and shifted into his wolf to join her.

PART III:
THE BATTLE BEGINS

Faces stay hidden in the shadows,
A figure stays hidden from the light,
Whispers of a name long forgotten
Flicker like embers through the night.

An angry hiss echoes all around me
In this icy cavern, dark as night.
The figure now beckons from a doorway,
And from inside shineth a dull light.

At my approach the figure sets upon me,
Pressing down on me with all his might.
I press back, he falters, and then…
My thoughts are startled ravens taking flight.

Chapter 14

As planned, they approached the cottage from the rear. Sniffing the air, Maelona caught the scent of at least two demonkin as well as well as a couple of humans. Blaez scanned the perimeter, and Maelona stood on her hind legs to peek in through the nearest window. On the inside, the main living area was one big room. There was one doorway off to the right and, judging from the size of the building on the outside, Maelona guessed it was a small bedroom. From her vantage point, she could see two demonkin and what she assumed to be a mother and son. The human boy looked to have fifteen to sixteen years.

Maelona glanced to her left to see Blaez disappearing around the corner, but her attention was quickly pulled back inside by the deep, gravelly rasp that was particular to the demonkin. "Well, look here," it said. "Looks like our prey is walking right into our hands."

With that, the large, ugly demonkin strode out of the cottage toward Gareth, who had just left the cover of the forest. Maelona quickly shifted back into her human form since she was more accustomed to fighting this way and she did not want to alarm the humans. She dressed in her clothing, making sure to secure all her weapons in their proper places. By the time she was ready, the first demonkin was far enough away for her to sneak around to the front of the building and quietly make her way inside.

She entered noiselessly, and since the second demonkin was

busy goading the humans, it did not notice her enter.

"Thrak there is going to destroy your prince," the large, ugly beast the color of bedrock said to his captives. "Then when our emperor signals that the time is right, we are going to lay siege to the city. Once it is ours, all the people of Eastgate will be our slaves. If you show your worth to me now, I may keep you as servants of my household, maybe even as my own personal pets."

"It is ironic that you are talking to your prisoners about worth," Maelona cut in from behind the demonkin, "when you yourself are so worthless."

The demonkin jumped up with a start and turned to face Maelona. She knew she needed to get it outside, away from the humans and into an area where she had more room to maneuver. She pulled her short sword from its sheath with one hand, and she turned her other hand palm up. With a taunting smirk on her lips, she beckoned to the demonkin and stepped back out through the doorway. As expected, the demonkin followed her.

This demonkin was as tall as Blaez in his human form, but wider and more stoutly built. Its arms and legs were as thick as tree trunks. This particular type of demonkin had skin that tended to be varying colors of grey to black, and just about as tough as the rock it looked like. Maelona was stronger and heavier than a human female her size would be, as seer muscles were denser. However, she knew that in a fight with such a creature she could not rely solely on overpowering him. The best plan of attack would be to outmaneuver and outsmart him.

She moved back away from the door a few more feet, then stood her ground as the demonkin came for her. She stood completely still until the demonkin was just in striking distance, then as its hand stretched out toward her in a punch, she dodged, pushing its punching arm to the side at the elbow. From there she stepped backward and then forward in a three-hundred-and-sixty-degree turn until she was behind it. Then she struck out with her sword across the back of its leg, severing the hamstring with one stroke.

However, demonkin themselves tended to be as tough as their hide, so the demonkin managed to stay on its feet, even with only one leg to support it. It dragged itself around to face her again, but before the beast even made it all the way around, she struck it with a vicious side kick: Swinging her back leg forward and around so it was parallel to the ground, her knee close to her chest, she then pushed her leg out with all her might as she let out an angry yell. The heel of her foot made contact with the demonkin's sternum and kept on pushing at a high velocity. The demonkin doubled over as all the air was forced from its lungs. Maelona then turned her back to the demonkin and looked over her shoulder at her target before she brought her knee up and pushed her foot back, connecting with a powerful back kick to the demonkin's face.

Before the demonkin even hit the ground, Maelona spotted movement in her peripheral vision. Looking to her right, she saw another demonkin running toward her from the cottage. There must have been another in the room with the closed door.

Before Maelona had time to react, however, a great, black form flew by her. Blaez, in wolf form, jumped onto the back of her demonkin, which had turned itself over onto its hands and knees, and pushed against the beast as he launched himself toward the newcomer.

Trusting Blaez to take care of himself, she turned her attention back to her opponent, who was now face down in the dirt from the force of Blaez leaping from its back. Maelona nudged it with her foot until it rolled onto its back. "Sit up," she ordered.

The demonkin slowly brought itself to a sitting position. Maelona grabbed its tunic at the shoulder to help it move faster. As they moved, Blaez, still in wolf form, pulled the other demonkin behind Maelona by the throat. Its neck was bloodied and mangled, and its head was hanging at an unnatural angle; clearly, the neck had been broken. Blaez dropped the body in direct sight of the other demonkin.

Though Maelona did not have her sword pointed directly at the demonkin, she held it at the ready, just in case the creature got any ideas. "Who sent you here?" she asked forcefully. "Who is behind this invasion?"

"That is no concern of yours," the demonkin replied.

Maelona pressed her blade against the carotid artery at the side of its neck until she drew surface blood. "Does it concern me now?" she asked.

The demonkin gave her the answer she asked for without really giving her any new information. "The emperor," he replied.

"And who, exactly, is this emperor?"

"You will find out soon enough," came the answer. "When he comes, he will rain destruction down upon all who try to resist him."

The demonkin continued to regard her with an icy stare. Maelona shook her head and tsked.

"And I suppose he promised you a share in his riches? Perhaps a castle and females and whatever other luxuries you desire?" The demonkin did not respond, but instead continued to glare at her.

Maelona began slowly pacing back and forth in front of the demonkin, shaking her head as if she felt sorry for it. "I am sorry to have to tell you this, but you are the first evil minions I have come across. The creatures relegated to the front lines. Do you know what this means?" she asked, looking at its face again. When the demonkin did not respond, she continued. "This means you are fodder to your emperor. Completely expendable. I could end you right now, and he would not even blink." The demonkin tried to appear unaffected, but Maelona noticed it swallow, and blink, at her words.

She paused for effect and then turned to him again. "You are lucky today, however. I am feeling generous. So, if you would like to share some information about your leader, perhaps I might let you li…"

The final word was not even uttered when the flash of a blade sliced through the demonkin's neck and his head went rolling to the ground. Maelona had heard human footsteps approaching and expected that it would be one of the hostages. What she didn't expect when she looked up, however, was a dirty, disheveled man who looked like he had undergone days of torture at the hands of his enemies.

While Maelona had made her way inside to confront the demonkin there and free the humans, Blaez had followed the scent of human blood and sweat until he found himself in the root cellar. There, he found a man hanging by ropes that were attached to the ceiling and tied around his wrists. The man's feet were touching the ground, but Blaez could only imagine the difficulty of his position when he couldn't stand any longer and was forced to rest.

The single demonkin present was preoccupied with picking out its next implement of torture when Blaez quietly arrived. When the beast finally noticed another presence there with them, it just looked at Blaez, clearly confused. Blaez used this hesitation to his advantage, quickly dispatching of the demonkin and switching to his human form so he could free the man from his restraints. As beat up and weak as the human looked, he managed to make his way up from the root cellar, grabbing a sword from the demonkin's corpse on the way.

Blaez followed him up the steps. Then, looking toward where Maelona was fighting another demonkin, he saw a third emerge through the doorway of the cottage. He took off running, shifting back to his wolf mid-stride. Using Maelona's now downed opponent as a springboard, he launched himself at the demonkin in the doorway. His jaws landed unerringly around his intended target - the demonkin's throat. Blaez felt bones crunch and flesh tear as he shook his great head, and when the body went limp, he brought it over and dropped it directly behind Maelona. He hoped it could be used as incentive to get the demonkin she was now questioning to talk.

Noticing movement behind Maelona's captive, Blaez looked up to see the man he had rescued come up behind the demonkin that was now sitting on the ground in front of Maelona. When Blaez realized what the man was doing, he hesitated, thinking the man had earned his right to retribution. Then it was too late for him to shift to human form to warn Maelona. The demonkin's victim brought the sword up and across with much more force than Blaez would have expected, given his physical state.

Blood spattered all around as the sword cut through the demonkin's neck, splashing onto Maelona's clothes and boots. She didn't even flinch at the bloody mess, which led Blaez to wonder just how many battles she had seen in the forty or so years since she first left the shifter village.

Finally, after expending the last of his energy beheading one of his tormentors, the man's strength failed him; he faltered, and then he fell unconscious to the ground.

Just then, Maelona heard Gareth's footsteps approaching from the left, and the female's footsteps from the right. The woman dropped to her knees next to the unconscious man and began to weep. Maelona turned to Blaez, still in wolf form, and said, "Leighis leaf." Blaez gave her a quick nod and took off back around the house.

Maelona moved around the body of the demonkin and kneeled next to the unconscious man. Looking at who she assumed was his wife, she said in a soft voice, "Let me help him." The woman paused and looked Maelona in the eye for a quick moment before nodding her consent.

"Here, let me help you," Gareth said. But he had barely taken a step forward when Maelona scooped the man into her arms as if he were a small child and carried him into the house. Gareth stood stunned for a moment, but then followed behind her.

Gareth had just stepped inside the cottage when Blaez entered, in human form and fully dressed, carrying both his and Maelona's packs. "That was fast," Gareth commented.

Maelona accepted her pack from Blaez and reached inside for her pouch of leighis leaf.

"I found the man restrained in the root cellar," Blaez said. "I let him loose. I wouldn't have guessed he could behead a demonkin in his state."

Maelona nodded her agreement. "The human spirit is strong," she said.

She turned to Gareth. "I need you to start a fire for me, then boil some water." Then she turned her attention back to the woman. "What is your name?" she asked, her voice soft with compassion.

"Laoise," the woman responded.

"And your husband?"

"Teague. My son," she added, nodding toward the boy, who now sat by the hearth, "is named Withell."

Maelona looked at the boy and noticed he was covered in bruises and scratches. She felt a flash of rage at the thought of what the demonkin had done to this family. She pushed it aside for the moment, however, so she could focus on caring for Teague.

"Well, Laoise, your husband will be fine. He has suffered some trauma, and he looks to be dehydrated and malnourished, but he is in no immediate danger. We cannot stay beyond an hour or so, unfortunately, so I will teach you how to care for him and, if you follow my instructions, he will be fine."

"Okay," Laoise responded. Her responses so far were short, and she still shivered. Maelona worried that she was in a state of shock, and hoped that giving her a task to complete would help her come around.

Maelona emptied the contents of the pouch into her hand. Showing it to Laoise, she said, "This is leighis leaf. It is a wonder of nature. It can heal almost any injury or illness from the inside and from the outside. I will show you how to prepare it. This will help Teague to heal much faster."

Laoise nodded and listened intently as Maelona explained how to prepare the compresses to place on his external injuries, then how to prepare the tea.

"As soon as he is conscious and able, have him drink as much as he will take," Maelona instructed her. Maelona prepared the leaf as she had instructed while Laoise watched on.

As they waited for the tea and compresses to be ready, Maelona gave some more advice to Laoise. "If you need more leighis leaf, you can find it in the Sacred Forest."

"In th—the forest?" Laoise asked nervously.

"Yes," Maelona answered. "You need not fear the forest. It is only dangerous to any evil beings that enter, despite what you may have heard. The leighis tree is a very tall tree, with green leaves all over except for at the very top. It is capped with dark red leaves. Both the green and the red leaves have healing properties, though the red tend to be stronger." Laoise nodded her understanding.

"Also," Maelona continued, "I do not believe any more demonkin will make it back this far, but if they do, take your family and head into the forest. There are those in the forest who are always willing to help someone in need. If they question you, tell them Maelona Sima sent you." Maelona had no doubt that, after the meeting with the elders, her name was becoming well-known to those who lived in the Sacred Forest.

Laoise was looking at her with a mix of disbelief and fear, so Maelona went to her pack and reached into a small pocket near the bottom. She removed an amulet similar to the one Gareth had been wearing when she and Blaez found him. Before she moved it into Laoise's line of sight, however, she clasped her hands around it for a moment. A lavender glow shone briefly, visible where her hands came together. Then she turned to Laoise and placed the amulet around her neck.

"Wear this," she told Laoise, "and my people will know who sent you." Amulets were usually given sparingly by the seer elders to trusted friends, but given the current circumstances in the realm, Maelona had taken a few with her, just in case. Maelona looked Laoise in the eye and added, "Trust me." Laoise must have been satisfied with what she saw in Maelona, as her shoulders relaxed and she nodded her agreement.

Maelona had kept an eye on Laoise while they prepared the medicine and waited for it to be ready. She was satisfied that Laoise no longer seemed as though she would go into shock. Laoise had shown real interest in learning how to heal, limited though the time allowed it to be. She also began talking more animatedly with Maelona, explaining how they had become captive to the demonkin.

"Withell had been working the small field between the cottage and the road," Laoise told Maelona, "and had noticed Gareth as he passed through. Of course, we did not know his name at the time," she added. "but Withell told us he was dressed as if he were someone of importance. Withell noticed as well that three demonkin followed Gareth down the path and into the forest not too long afterward. When he came inside that day, he told us about what he had seen. Then, a couple of days later, three new demonkin arrived, barged into our home, and demanded to be provided with food and shelter while they waited for the others to return.

"Teague had tried to fight them off, and was beaten for his efforts, right in front of us." Laoise's eyes began to tear up as she recounted this part of the story. "Withell had tried to jump in at one point. I tried to hold him back, but he was determined to help his father. The demonkin just tossed him aside as if he were a sack of feathers." Laoise shook her head and swallowed back a sob. "Teague fought valiantly and held his own for a while. In the end, though, the three demonkin overpowered him. They beat him until he was barely holding onto consciousness, then one of the demonkin dragged him outside. My son and I did not see him again until today. We didn't know if he was alive or dead."

Laoise was visibly shaking again by the time she was done her story. Maelona placed her hand on Laoise's back and rubbed small circles to help soothe her. Then she told Laoise, "You are safe now."

An hour or so after they began, the medicines were administered and Maelona had given Laoise instructions on how often to change the compresses and administer the tea.

Now Maelona put on her pack and headed out the front door, where Gareth and Blaez were standing guard after disposing of the demonkin bodies. Movement caught Maelona's attention as Withell, who had been sitting next to Blaez, stood up to face her.

"I want to thank you for helping my family today," he said. "I was so scared. We hadn't seen Father in three days, and I thought the demonkin were either going to eat us or carry us off to be slaves."

"You are very welcome," Maelona said warmly. "I am glad you are all okay." Her eyes scanned the youth's face with concern. "It was very brave of you to try and help your father," she said. "Place some compresses on your injuries as well. It will help them heal faster."

Maelona looked at Withell thoughtfully for a moment. She swung her pack around to the front and again reached into the small pocket. She took out another amulet. This time she didn't try to hide it as she held the amulet between her cupped palms and closed her eyes. Rays of lavender light peeked out where her hands came together once again. When it was done, she opened her eyes and looked at Withell.

"I want you to wear this at all times," she said as she placed the amulet around his neck. "It will keep you safe." Placing her hand on his shoulder, she met his eyes and added, "stay close to your parents until the coming dark times have passed. When you are ready, come find me, and I will teach you how to protect yourself and your family."

Withell looked at her, eyes wide in awe. "Are you a sorceress?" he asked.

"Among other things," she responded. "But that part must not be mentioned to anyone else for the time being, you understand."

He nodded once at her in response, at a loss for words.

Then, turning to look over her shoulder at Laoise, Maelona said, "Don't forget, you will always have friends in the Sacred Forest if you are willing to accept them." Then she nodded to Blaez and Gareth, and they headed off down the path to the road.

Once they were out of earshot of the humans, Gareth asked Maelona, "What was that thing you did, with the purple light?"

"Protection spell," Maelona replied.

"Pfftt! Why didn't your father think to put one of those on the amulet he gave my father?" Gareth asked rhetorically. "It could have saved me from some pain and suffering, not to mention healing time, when I was attacked by those three demonkin."

"Maybe Maddock foresaw you needed some tough love to help you become a man," Blaez said, deadpan.

"If I need some tough love to help me become a man," Gareth retorted, "maybe Maelona here should be the one to give it to me." He waggled his eyebrows at Blaez, and Blaez growled at him in return.

Maelona shook her head and sped up her pace to walk on ahead of them. She still heard Gareth, however, when he asked Blaez, "How do you do that growly thing when you're in human form, anyway?"

Chapter 15

Maelona, Blaez, and Gareth kept walking until the moon shone bright overhead. Maelona and Blaez had rested just the night before and, because of their species, they would not rest again this night. Gareth, however, was human. He tried to insist that he was fine to keep going through the night. However, Maelona had seen the scenarios they might encounter and needed him to be at his best. She would not tell him this, of course, so to make him feel a little better about giving in and sleeping, she convinced him she had some matters to attend to.

"Go ahead and get some rest, Gareth," she said. "I need to clean and sharpen my weapons, and this will be a good opportunity to do so. In fact, hand me your weapons, and I will clean and sharpen them as well."

This was true, to a degree. While her weapons were still in good condition, she didn't know when she would have a chance to take care of them again, and she liked her weapons to be in top condition for a battle. So, she figured this may be the best opportunity she would have before the storm that was to come.

She and Blaez moved a short distance from where Gareth lay sleeping. They were close enough to hear if any wild animal or enemy came upon him as he slept, but far enough that the sounds of metal against metal and stone would not wake him.

They set about their tasks in companionable silence. Blaez could not help but look Maelona's way from time to time, and he could tell she was going over something in her mind.

After a time, Maelona spoke up, saying, "If you shift from wolf to human during battle, make sure to grab the first weapon that you see since you won't be able to carry one in wolf form."

"I will," he responded.

Then she continued sharpening her blade. A short time later, she again spoke up out of the blue. "Maybe we should have Gareth practice with us more. He plants his feet too much. He is so much smaller than some of the beasts we will be battling. He can't count on strength alone to get him through what's to come."

Blaez got up from the stump he had been sitting on, turned to Maelona, and held out his hand to her. When she hesitated, he said, "Come." With that, she lay down the dagger she had been sharpening and took his hand. He led her over to a patch of grass, where they both lay down on their backs gazing up at the stars. It reminded him of another night not so long ago, though it felt like a lifetime ago.

Blaez reached across to grasp Maelona's hand in his. He took a deep breath in, inhaling the fresh scent of the clean air. Maelona did the same. Then Blaez began to speak.

"I know and understand how useful, life-saving even, seers' visions can be. But at times like tonight, I can see how they can be a curse as well." He turned his head to the side to look at her as he continued. "You can't do this to yourself, my Lona. I don't know what you have seen, but you have said that the future is always shifting."

"Some things do shift, but there are also things that will stay the same," she interjected. "And sometimes I wish I could see things that I can't."

"It does no good for you to spend all of your time worrying about what may come and being blind to what you have in the present," Blaez said.

Shaking her head, she said, "I do understand that, Blaez. Logically, in my mind, I understand. But I've been having a difficult time staying rational and neutral, as I had always been in the past. Sometimes it seems as though, now that I am allowing myself to feel my emotions, I feel *too* much. Now that I have allowed you and Gareth in, especially you, I feel like I have so much more to lose."

"You need to trust us to be able to take care of ourselves."

"I do, Blaez," Maelona asserted. "Honestly I do. But it's been a long time since I've dealt with my emotions. It's been a long time since I have done anything more than deny them, locking them away deep inside. It's been a long time since I let anyone in, and now I fear the possibility of losing what I've gained." She took a deep breath before adding, "It just feels a little overwhelming."

Then, turning her head to meet his gaze, she said, "Don't worry, mo grá. I will learn to moderate my emotions, but it may take some time." *I just hope I can learn this before I need to use my magic,* she added to herself.

The trio was up and on their way again at sunrise the next morning. As they walked, Maelona noticed that Gareth wasn't his chipper and annoying self.

"Is there something on your mind this morning, Gareth?"

Gareth looked at her, his expression unsure, as if he didn't know if he wanted to say anything or not. She was glad when he spoke again, glad he chose to share.

"I keep thinking that it's my fault that the demonkin attacked that family. The beasts wouldn't have been there at all if they hadn't been following me."

"You know," Maelona replied, "my mother and I had a similar discussion about something that happened in the past. Do you want to know the conclusion I came to?"

"Please," he replied.

"We cannot blame ourselves for the actions of others. Everyone has choices. The dark sorcerer chose to send the demonkin after you. The demonkin chose to follow his orders. They decided to hold that family captive and torture them. Then you chose to help Blaez and me fight back against them and free Laoise, Teague, and Withell. You made the right choices. It was those beasts who made the wrong ones."

About an hour out from where they had camped for the

night, they could see smoke billowing in the air. It seemed to be coming from just past the next rise. Soon, they were cresting the hill, and what they saw on the other side twisted their stomachs.

At the top of the hill, they stopped to take in the destruction that lay not more than a few meters in front of them. A burnt-out husk of a farmer's cottage stood as the backdrop to a pile of charred remains, which looked to be all that was left of three or four people.

"Universe, help us," Gareth said as they looked at what remained of this innocent family. Smoke billowed up around them as the wind gusted through.

"I have never smelled burning human flesh before. I think the stench is soaking into my clothes."

"It is not a smell I will forget anytime soon," Blaez commented.

"How could anyone do such a thing to innocent people?" Gareth commented.

"You would be surprised what some would do for power and wealth," Maelona said.

They had started to move forward slowly again, looking around to check for survivors, when Maelona suddenly said, "I have a confession to make."

"Okay," Gareth said, drawing out the word.

Without waiting for further acknowledgment, she continued, "I love fighting. Especially hand to hand."

"And is this a bad thing?" Gareth queried.

Maelona glanced over at Gareth. "It is not the seer way," she answered. "We learn to fight because we are protectors of the light. Protectors of the realm and all that is innocent and good in it. We learn to be very skilled at what we do because it is our duty. Fighting and killing others, even when they are evil beings who harm the innocent, is not something to be done lightly. These are actions seen as necessary, but regrettable."

She let out a small laugh as a memory came to her. "My trainer, Donogh Carr, used to get annoyed with me for smiling while we sparred. He would say, 'Fighting is a serious matter, Maelona!'" she said, while trying to imitate his voice.

"But it's not the killing of others I enjoy," she added while shaking her head. "It's the beauty and artistry behind the fight. It's watching your opponent for subtle hints of what they will do next, and the feeling of accomplishment you get when you are victorious because you anticipated correctly. It's how the two combatants move together, back and forth, as they attack and defend and counter-attack. It's almost like a dance."

"That is a beautiful image," Blaez commented.

Maelona glanced over at him. Her voice became stronger as she repeated, "It was never the killing of others that I enjoyed.

"However," she continued, the threat evident in her voice, "when I find those responsible for this atrocity, I will thoroughly enjoy making them pay."

Chapter 16

The closer Gareth, Maelona, and Blaez got to Eastgate, the more populated with cottages the area became. Yet there was no human life to be found.

They came across numerous other burnt-out shells and a few other bodies as they went forward. However, there were some intact homes that seemed abandoned as well.

"Where are all the people?" Gareth asked. "The number of bodies we've seen is only a small portion of our population."

"I can only assume the inhabitants were either captured or fled," Maelona answered.

As they approached the castle town of Eastgate, they veered off the main road and into the woods.

"We need to keep the element of surprise as much as possible," Maelona had explained, "and take in the state of things in the town before heading to the castle."

When they were close to the treeline, they crouched low to the ground and looked out onto the town, scanning for any hidden dangers.

As with the other homes they had passed, smoke and ash rose up into the air and swirled all around, but they could detect no movement otherwise. Houses were nothing but ruins on the ground. The corpses of several companion animals lay strewn in the street. Straight ahead, the marketplace was nothing but rubble. Fires still burned, and what wasn't burning, smoldered.

"Where is everyone?" Gareth asked. "Where are the

demonkin? The town is a mess, but the castle does not seem to have been breached."

"The demonkin are hiding behind that ridge," Maelona answered, lifting her chin to indicate the hill line to the north-west of the castle. She had seen many of these sights in her dream-visions, though there was still much that fluctuated in her more recent ones.

Maelona took in the sight before her for a time and then turned to look at Gareth. "Is there another way into the castle, Gareth? A secret way? Preferably one that is hard to detect?"

"Yes," he answered. "Follow me."

The castle town extended in a circle all around the castle proper, and the area beyond the town was mostly wooded. Gareth led Maelona and Blaez through the woods and around to the side of the castle. He stopped in front of what appeared to be a rock sitting in front of a small hill. Moving behind the rock, he pushed aside a curtain of moss and vines and said, "Through here."

Instead of entering the hidden tunnel, Maelona turned to look at Blaez. As if he read her mind, he said, "The others should be here by now. I will shift and head off to meet with them."

"Tell them to stay hidden in the forest until after the battle begins," Maelona said. "I want them to watch the perimeter of the castle and to stay behind the enemy. I am hoping we can take the demonkin and their army by surprise.

"I don't think they'll be expecting seers and shifters to be fight-ing alongside the humans. Not with our history. This should give us an advantage. We will draw them in, letting them think they have gained the upper hand. Then, when the time is right, the shifters will come in behind the enemy, leaving them no means of escape."

"Agreed," Blaez responded. He turned to leave.

"Wait," Maelona said, grabbing Blaez's arm and swinging him around to face her again.

"When you know that the others are set to act, come back here to this tunnel and find me inside the castle. I will need you by my side."

Blaez smiled affectionately at Maelona, reaching to cup her cheek in his large hand. "Until then, stay safe, mo grá," he said. He dipped his head to give her a brief, chaste kiss.

"And you as well," she responded, placing her own hand over his briefly. Then Blaez turned and ran back the way they had come. A moment later, they heard a wolf howl, followed by an answering howl.

"Good," Maelona commented. "They're here."

When she turned to face Gareth, he gestured to the tunnel and said, "Let's go."

"We're not going that way," Maelona stated, her voice immediately harder. "I just wanted Blaez to know the way. We are going through the town."

"What? Why would you want to do that?" Gareth asked, alarmed. "We'll be completely exposed out there. You may as well paint targets on our backs."

"We need to check for survivors," she responded. "And I think for the most part they'll stay hidden. They have pulled back to wait for reinforcements."

"How could you possibly know tha—" Gareth started. Then, remembering, he added, "Oh, never mind."

Gareth and Maelona headed through the town in the direction of the castle. As they walked, they saw a number of dead, comprised of the good people of Eastgate as well as their enemies, the demonkin. "I thought it was said at the fire circle that others were working with the evil sorcerer. Snowbeasts and the like," Gareth remarked. "Why are we only seeing demonkin?"

"They are doing as we are," she replied. "Hiding their numbers, trying to take us by surprise. Also, they will be saving their strongest forces to take the Great Gate, which is why we asked Taranis and Brennus to meet us there."

"Lucky we have you then," he said. "It's hard to take a seer by surprise."

Maelona didn't respond this time. When he glanced over at her, he could see the barely concealed tension and anger in her expression. The closer they got to the castle and the more bodies they passed, the worse it got. It was like he could feel the anger rolling off her in waves.

Gareth looked at Maelona and was about to make a comment when he saw movement out of the corner of his eye.

"Watch out!" he yelled.

But, it turns out he needn't have worried. When the arrow that was headed straight at Maelona's back got within a couple of feet of her, it slowed down almost to a stop. He watched as it then disintegrated in front of his eyes, from the tip out to the end.

Maelona hadn't even flinched.

Gareth gaped at Maelona in shock, which quickly changed to awe. "Is there something you've neglected to tell me, my friend?" he asked. When Maelona didn't answer, he added, "Remind me not to get on your bad side."

A couple of minutes later, Gareth heard Maelona speaking quietly, angrily, almost as if she were talking to herself. "So much life lost," she said. "And for what? For one man's greed and his quest for power."

By now they had reached the gatehouse, and they paused as the bridge descended and the portcullis opened. When they entered, the soldiers at the gate bowed to Gareth, saying, "Your Highness."

As they walked through the outer bailey, Gareth was relieved to see that a great number of the kingdom's people had made it to safety inside the castle walls. The outer bailey was set up as a temporary camp. There were even some merchants selling food and the like.

They had just walked through the gate to the inner bailey when they heard a feminine voice say, "Welcome home, brother."

At the sound of her voice, Maelona turned to look at Gareth's sister, who looked to be a couple of years younger than him. She was a stunning young woman with hazel eyes and dark auburn hair that tumbled in waves to mid-back.

Gareth was taken by surprise when, before he had a chance to speak, much of the tension seemed to leave Maelona, and she stepped forward with a genuine, warm smile on her face. This was a significant difference from just a few minutes ago, outside.

"You are Maeve, daughter of Niall, King of Eastgate."

Maeve could not help but return the smile as she said, "I am.

And who might you be?"

"I am Maelona Sima, daughter of Maddock Sima, who was a friend of your father's."

"Yes, I know who he is. Father has spoken of him often," Maeve responded. Then, with a sense of urgency, she added, "Come, I will take you to him."

The three of them headed to the staircase at a hurried pace, but when they reached the bottom, Maelona paused and turned toward a darkened hallway to their right.

"What are you doing?" Gareth asked her. But before she could respond, a figure emerged and walked toward them.

Maelona smiled widely and nodded her greeting. "Blaez," she said, reaching her hand out to grasp his for a moment.

"Well, that was quick," Gareth commented.

"Yes, it seems I can move much faster when I don't have to pace myself to match a sluggish human," Blaez returned.

Ignoring the men, Maeve said to Maelona, "Father has been waiting for you. Actually, he's been waiting for Maddock, but I am sure he'll be glad you are here." In a worried tone, she added, "He has not been well."

As they reached the door to the king's chambers, they passed a guard who was posted outside. Maelona cut a sideways glance, taking him in quickly before entering the room.

They all paused and waited just inside the doorway for a moment. Maelona turned to make sure it was shut and locked.

"He's been very weak," Maeve said, sending a concerned look in the king's direction. "He has lost a lot of weight and has been sleeping for longer and longer periods. Let me just go and tell him you are here."

As Maeve walked away, Maelona removed her braid to leave her hair loose down her back.

Maeve approached her father's bed quietly. Shaking his shoulder very gently, she said, "Father, you have a visitor."

"Who is it?" he asked in a weak, raspy voice.

Before Maeve could answer him, Maelona responded, "It is I, old friend." As she walked toward the king's bed, her hair color changed from root out to tip. Audible gasps could be heard from the others in the room, except the king.

For Gareth and Maeve, they looked shocked and surprised. Blaez, on the other hand, was rather awed, for standing before them now was the most magnificent creature he had ever seen.

Maelona's natural hair color was white-blonde at the roots, very subtly blending to pale lavender and then gradually growing darker until it was a much richer lavender at the ends. The shift in color reminded him of the petals of a flower he had once seen in the Sacred Forest.

As she moved forward toward the bed, she glanced over at Blaez, and he saw the same bright violet eyes he had seen when she had changed to her wolf form. Her skin was slightly darker too, he noticed, which made the color of her hair and eyes stand out even more. Of course, she had always been exceptional in his eyes, but in her natural form she truly stood out amongst women. Now he realized why he had not remembered seeing her around the village as a child. She would have been in her natural colors and would have looked quite different.

Once she reached the king's bedside, Maelona smiled down at him. Smiling back, he said, "Maelona Sima! You are a sight for sore, old eyes. How long has it been? Forty, fifty years?"

"Something like that," she replied.

"Well, it would seem that you have aged much better than I have," he quipped.

Maelona laughed lightly at that. Then, still smiling, she said, "Your daughter tells me you haven't been feeling well."

"No, not for a month or more, probably, though it has gotten worse of late."

"Well, let me take a look at you, old man."

The king laughed at that, saying, "I may look old, but let's not forget that you have a few years on me, my friend."

"That I do," she responded. Then, she placed her hands on his cheeks and pulled his lower eyelids down with her thumbs. Next, she looked at his mouth and lips. Finally, she took his hands in hers and examined his nails. Then, turning to the others she said, "Come closer, everyone."

They all gathered around the bed and looked at Maelona expectantly.

"King Niall has been poisoned," she said in a quiet voice. Gareth and Maeve gasped at this news. Then Maelona added, "It looks like this poisoning has been going on over a period of time. A few months, probably."

"But how is that possible?" Maeve asked. "My father is always guarded. His Royal Guard, who you saw outside the door, has been with my father for decades, and he always tastes my father's food and drink first."

"Well, the answer to the how," Maelona responded, "probably has much to do with the fact that the guard outside the door is not human. He is demonkin."

There were sharp intakes of breaths from all around at this news. Then Maeve asked, "We've had a demonkin on our staff for decades? How is that possible?"

Maelona shook her head and responded, "It's more likely that it killed your real guard so it could take his place."

Now very angry, Maeve practically growled out the words as she said, "I'm going to kill him! I'm going to tear him apart with my bare hands!"

"Let's wait on that a bit," Maelona responded calmly. "I may be able to use the creature to gather some more information."

"Okay, let's get back to the important stuff," Gareth stated impatiently. "Is Father going to be okay?"

Maelona gave him a warm, compassionate smile as she answered, "Yes, he will be. I can help him, but we have no time to waste." Turning to address the king she added, "What I have seen in my visions would suggest that the attack will happen in the next day or two. Possibly even as early as tomorrow." Looking back at the others she said, "We need him to get well before then."

"Maybe we should just have him sit this one out," suggested Gareth softly.

Maelona could hear the worry in his tone, so she gave him

a small smile of understanding as she replied, "I'm afraid that won't be possible, Gareth. We seers consider ourselves to be guardians of the realm, but I also have a more specific task, as does your father. We are the guardians of Eastgate, tasked with protecting the keystone."

King Niall's expression turned sad as he looked at Maelona and asked, "So your father…?"

Nodding, she said, "Probably not more than six or seven years after your visit." Looking back at the others, she explained, "Guardianships are passed down from parent to child for the humans. They are sometimes passed the same way for seers, but not always.

"Our fathers protected Eastgate when King Niall and I were young, but with their passing, the honor, and the responsibility, fall to us. Actually, I insisted on taking my father's place, though they made me train for some years before allowing it. They appointed another seer warrior until I was ready."

Taking off her pack, she dug around for a moment before pulling out a pouch. Looking to the hearth, she said, "Gareth, start a fire." He nodded and set to work.

Maelona continued, "Maeve, you will need to heat some water." Maeve moved to grab the pitcher of water on the table near her father's bed. "Wait," Maelona said. Taking the pitcher, she smelled the water, then poured a small amount into one of the cups and tasted it. "The water is fine," she announced. "It must have been the food that was poisoned."

She handed the pitcher of water to Maeve, who then poured it into a small pot and placed it over the fire Gareth had started.

"The leighis tea will help you heal, but it will take too long. So, I will try to help it along," she said.

Maelona had never attempted what she was going to try now, and she was nervous. Though she tried to hide it, her hand shook slightly and her voice subtly quavered.

As if Blaez could sense Maelona's nervousness and wanted to show her his support and confidence in her without being obvious, he walked over and stood close to her. He said, "I will prepare the leighis leaf for the tea."

As he took the pouch from her, he let his large hand linger around her smaller one for a moment, giving it a reassuring squeeze. At the same time, he caught her gaze and gave her a little nod. Looking back into his eyes, she returned his nod in a silent thank you to him.

Chapter 17

As Blaez headed over to the fire with the others, Maelona returned her attention to the king. "Well, Niall," she said, "It's been a long time since I have tried anything like this." *Actually,* she thought, *I have never tried anything exactly like this.*

Before she had left the shifters to take her father's place with the seers, her mother had tried to teach her some healing spells. She hadn't gotten very far. But she was a seer as well as a sorceress, and once she had committed herself to the seer ways, she began to learn how to focus her abilities inwards. Her father had taught her how to manipulate the elements within her body to change hair and eye color before he went to the other side, and it hadn't taken her long with the seers to figure out how to use this ability for healing as well.

She wasn't sure why, but her instincts now told her that she could use her magic to enable her to focus this Inner Sight, as the seers called it, into the body of another. She hoped to be able to use it to help heal Niall.

"I trust you, Maelona," the king said. "I have faith in you."

With that, Maelona placed one hand on King Niall's forehead and another on his abdomen and, closing her eyes, she focused her mind inward. She could see inside her own physical form. She could see all the molecules of matter, and she could feel her life force. Then she called upon her power, bringing it forth to form a bridge between her own body and Niall's. She followed its path as it traveled through his physical form until she found the molecules of the chemical used to poison the king. When she was certain she had isolated all the toxin, she then used her mind and her magic to obliterate it into nothingness.

She opened her eyes as the pale lavender light of her magic faded from sight. She looked down at Niall and, with surprise, said, "Wow. I'm better at that than I thought."

Maeve and Gareth came forward to check on their father. "What did you do?" Maeve asked, awe evident in her voice.

"I healed him," Maelona answered simply.

"But he looks even better than he did before," Maeve stated. "He looks ten or fifteen years younger than he did before he took ill."

"I can only assume that the magic flowing through his body had the same effect on him as it does on sorcerers," Maelona explained. "It is our magic that causes sorcerers to age more slowly than others of our species because it renews our cells as it flows through us."

"But your mother healed my leg," Gareth said, "and I still look the same."

Maelona shook her head as she tried to puzzle it out. "Maybe it's because she had localized her magic to your injuries, whereas I had to spread mine throughout your father's body to find and destroy all the molecules of the toxin. Or maybe it's because my powers are different from hers."

King Niall swung his legs over the bed and stood to his full height. "Well, it is a very lovely side-effect," he said, "but we should save the 'whys' for another time. We have some strategizing to do."

Leaning toward Maelona, Gareth said under his breath, in an effort to be discreet, "A couple of decades from now, I'll be asking you to do that for me." Maelona couldn't help but grin.

"First things first," Niall continued, looking to Maelona, "we have a demonkin posing as my Royal Guard. We need to find out if it's the only one to have infiltrated the castle. Most importantly, we need to find out if the keystone has been tampered with."

Maelona nodded her agreement at the same time as Maeve

asked, "How are we going to do that?"

"Just like this," Niall said, striding to the door and swinging it open. Maelona quickly switched her coloring back to her customary browns.

The guard turned to look at the king, then took a step back in surprise. "My l—lord! H—how?" he stammered.

"Step inside my chamber, and we will tell you all about it," the king stated. He moved to the side to allow the imposter to enter. Once he was inside, the king closed and locked the door again, then stood in front of it, just in case the demonkin decided to try to make a run for it. Maelona couldn't help but smile at Niall as she thought to herself that her old friend had not lost any of his boldness with age.

The guard looked from the king to the others before saying, "What is this about?"

"I have some questions for you," the king stated. "And if you value your life, you will answer them truthfully. First of all, I want you to tell me what you did with Drest."

"What are you talking about? I am Drest," the demonkin answered with a confused look on its face. If Maelona were not a seer, naturally skilled at detecting falsehoods in others, she might have been convinced it was being genuine.

The king pulled a dagger from a sheath at his waist.

"Did you have that dagger on you in your sick bed?" Blaez asked.

Niall just shrugged and said, "Being king is a dangerous profession, as you can see."

"I will ask you again," Niall said, pressing the tip of the dagger against the false guard's throat and pushing him up against the wall. "Where. Is. Drest?"

"I don't know what you're talking about, my lord," the demonkin replied.

The king sighed and shook his head. Moving the dagger away from the impostor's throat just long enough to gesture toward Maelona, he said, "You see my friend over there? She will be able to tell me without a shadow of a doubt whether you are lying or telling the truth."

The demonkin looked to Maelona, and she watched its eyes widen in realization. "How can you trust one such as her?" it spat. "Her race is tricky and deceitful! I am horrified to know that any survived!"

Maelona had tired of the game this creature was playing. She stepped forward and, looking into its eyes, she asked, "Shall I let them see what I see?"

Without giving it a moment to respond, she raised her hand and placed it against the pretender's chest. Her simple touch dissolved the illusion it had wrapped around itself, shattering the image of the guard and, in its place, leaving the disturbing reality of what lay underneath.

The demonkin's shape was roughly that of a large human, but that was where the similarities ended. Its skin was mottled red and pink, as though it was recovering from severe burns. Its facial structure looked distorted, pulled outward, and it had small horns all along its cheekbones that became larger and larger as they continued past its temples.

Letting go of the charade, the demonkin's demeanor suddenly changed from one of a nervous and confused guard to an angry and spiteful monster. "Do to me what you will, I will tell you nothing!" the demonkin spat.

"Make no mistake," Maelona spoke calmly, "you will tell me. You can either choose to do it the easy way and answer our questions, or you can do it the hard way, where I pull the answers from you. And I can promise you, that will not be pleasant for you."

"The likes of you has no power over me," the demonkin declared. "Soon you will all be crushed under our feet!"

"Okay," Maelona said with a sigh. "The hard way it is. So be it."

Maelona placed her hand against its forehead, and the demonkin suddenly stood still as if it were being pinned against the wall. The others watched on as her hand began to glow with a low, white and lavender light that soon became brighter and brighter. After what was probably no more than a few minutes, Maelona pulled her hand away and the body of the demonkin fell to the ground in a lifeless lump.

"Is it dead?" Maeve asked.

"No," Maelona replied, "but I can guarantee that it won't be doing much more than drooling from now on."

"Isn't that a little harsh?" Gareth asked, wincing.

"Well, I do not like to take life unnecessarily, but I also didn't want to take the chance of it escaping and tampering with the keystone while we are distracted with battle," she answered. "I can undo the effects if the need arises."

"Speaking of battle," Niall interjected, "let's stick to our first priorities. What did you learn, Maelona? Is Drest…?"

Maelona shook her head, a sad expression on her face.

King Niall look stricken for a moment. Maeve grabbed hold of his forearm in a show of support. Then Niall cleared his throat and said, "There will be time to mourn later. We need to focus on dealing with the current threats."

"I will begin with the things we need to take care of immediately," Maelona responded. "First of all, he was not the only demonkin placed in the castle. There are three others. There is one taking the place of a cook in the kitchen. Its job was to administer the poison in low doses over time to keep you weak and under control." The king made a growling sound at this but otherwise did not interrupt.

"The guard here," she continued, while gesturing to the unconscious form on the ground, "was to keep tabs on you and make sure you consumed your poisoned food. And the final two demonkin were tasked with finding a way to compromise the keystone."

"Were they successful?" the king asked, alarm evident in his tone.

"As of their last check-in with your friend here, no, they were not," she answered. "But I do suggest that our first order of business be finding the imposters and taking them out of the picture." King Niall nodded his agreement, and Maelona continued, "Blaez and I will take care of them. It shouldn't take us long. They don't know they've been discovered, so they shouldn't be difficult to catch off guard."

"Agreed," Niall said. "Meet us back here afterward, and you can tell us anything else you learn. If we are lucky, maybe you will discover something that will give us the upper hand in the coming battle."

As Maelona and Blaez left the room, they could hear Maeve saying, "I didn't know seers had those kinds of abilities."

"Normally, they don't," King Niall replied. The warmth and affection in his voice was evident as he continued, "But Maelona…is special."

Chapter 18

Maelona walked into the main kitchen and found who she was looking for right away. She found it amazing how the other humans milling about didn't notice anything different about the cook. It was a huge, demonkin male who was disguised as the short and plump cook. She looked around the room to see if the other demonkin were there, but all she saw was a couple of kitchen workers. She approached the demonkin.

"Are you the head cook?" Maelona asked.

"Yes, I am," it replied. "How can I help you?"

"I brought King Niall some special herbs to put in his meals to help him feel better." Maelona held a closed hand out to the fake cook, who looked down to see what she had. Maelona touched her other hand to the back of the poser's head, and its body stiffened before it went unconscious. Maelona lowered the limp form slowly to the ground.

There were gasps from the other kitchen staff once the illusion was dissolved and they realized they had been working with a demonkin. Maelona put a finger to her lips as she moved closer to the humans.

"There are two others," she said. "I do not want to alert them that we're on to them and looking for them." The staff nodded their heads in understanding.

"Do you have somewhere to hide the body until we get back to bring it to the dungeon?"

"Is it dead?" a female worker asked.

"No, just unconscious," Maelona said.

"What do we do if it wakes up?"

"It won't," Maelona replied.

"We have a large pantry back here," a male said. "We can hide it in here."

"Thank you," Maelona said before she and the male carried the huge form to its hiding spot.

Maelona and Blaez followed the staircase that led down into the keep. The staircase circled the whole outer circumference of the keep, which had been dug down to fifty feet underground. It was as if a stone tube encircled a stone tube, and between the two was a staircase.

When they reached the bottom, they paused so Maelona could explain the layout.

"The keep is not more than a couple of hundred feet wide, and anyone could guess that the keystone would be in the centre. So, it was designed like a labyrinth. Now that we're on the bottom level, we can walk all around the tunnel, and we will find six doors. Each of these doors have several narrow tunnels that lead in, with twists and turns that can deceive. We are not looking for the keystone, however. We are looking for those demonkin who are searching for it.

"So, this is where your wolf's nose comes in. There are two more demonkin, we know. We are looking for fresh scents to let us know they are down here. If they are, they will have probably split up to search faster. That means we should split up as well."

"Do you think that is wise, Maelona?" Blaez asked. "What if something happens?"

"Then we will deal with it. We will meet out here afterward, and the first one out will wait until the other shows. If the other doesn't show, then we will go looking. Agreed?"

"Agreed. Are you ready to shift again, Maelona?"

"I think so," she answered. "I will admit, I am a little nervous. I should have shifted more often to practice with the heightened senses, but there is no time to worry about that now."

They both stripped out of their clothing and placed it in their packs. Just before they shifted, Maelona said, "Blaez, try not to kill him if you don't have to. I know that will be harder for you in wolf form, but if you can manage it without endangering yourself, then keep him alive."

Blaez nodded, then stepped forward to place a soft kiss on her lips. He stepped back again, and his form shimmered and changed.

"Find the doors, Blaez, then I will open them and shift."

Blaez sniffed along the passageway as Maelona followed him. He paused and sniffed at all the doors before coming back to one he had checked a moment before. He yipped and looked from the door to Maelona. Then he walked a couple of doors over and yipped again. Maelona opened the doors and watched Blaez disappear inside one. She shifted to her wolf, took a moment to change to grey wolf coloring, then entered the other door.

It was dark inside the tunnels, but she could make out shapes. Soon, she realized she didn't need to rely on her sight anyway. She could hear every little scuffle of rodents and bugs, every scent from the stale smell of the dank earth under her feet to the smells of the small critters scurrying about.

She noticed one other scent as well. It was a foreign smell to her. It was neither pleasant nor unpleasant. It was earthy, yet different from the other earthy smells around her. It was like it was lightly scented with an unfamiliar spice.

Maelona knew instinctively that this was the smell she was looking for. When she came to a choice of three tunnels, she followed the scent to the left. She followed it again as it took a tunnel to the right. Finally, she saw a flicker of light around a corner not far ahead and heard an aggravated voice.

"Curse the human who made this cursed maze!" the voice said.

Maelona peeked around the corner to see that the demonkin male had come up against a dead end.

She stepped back and silently shifted back to her regular form. Rather than taking the time to re-dress, she decided to do as the demonkin did and created the illusion of clothing around herself. Then she stepped fully into the light of the demonkin's torch.

It was facing away from her, feeling along the wall. It had placed its torch in a sconce and was now using the hilt of a dagger to try to knock in stones in the wall. "There's got to be an easier way through this place," it muttered to itself.

"That won't work," Maelona said.

The demonkin started at the unexpected sound of a voice and turned around with its dagger at the ready.

"All the walls in here are magically reinforced," Maelona continued. "There is only one way through."

"Who are you?" the demonkin demanded.

"I'm an apparition," Maelona said. She smiled at the beast and took a step closer. The demonkin looked confused, like it wasn't sure what it should do in this situation.

Maelona wasn't sure if she could make it to the demonkin without it lunging at her with its weapon, so she sent some invisible tendrils of magic out ahead of her. If it attacked, its dagger would go the way of the arrow that had been sent in her direction earlier – dissolved into nothing.

"What do you want?" it asked as Maelona moved slowly forward toward it.

"Your thoughts," she replied, reaching out to touch her palm to its head. It stiffened suddenly at her touch, and while she learned what she could from it. Then she locked away the conscious parts of its mind, and it went limp.

When Maelona dragged the unconscious demonkin out of the tunnel, Blaez was already in the outer corridor. He was sitting, in wolf form, in front of a demonkin, growling in menacing tones. The demonkin watched Blaez warily until he spotted Maelona carrying his comrade's body out through the doorway.

"What did you do to him?" The demonkin barked. Blaez growled at him more loudly, but Maelona continued forward unfazed. She laid the unconscious form next to his buddy and then turned to face Blaez's prisoner.

"Don't worry, its nothing permanent," Maelona said. Then, without further warning, she placed her hand on its head and repeated the process of taking his thoughts and locking away his consciousness.

She reached out to Blaez and stroked his fur before saying, "Come on. Let's get dressed and get our prisoners to the dungeon.

The king and the others will be waiting for us."

Maelona watched as Blaez shifted back to his human form. Just as she was about to turn to get her clothing out of her pack, Blaez spoke.

"Maelona?"

"Yes?" she said as she turned back to face him.

"Are you sure they are unconscious? Oblivious to anything around them?"

"Most certainly," she replied.

"Then come here," he said. He reached for her and pulled her tight to him.

Maelona gasped as she felt her naked body press against his firm, taut form for the very first time.

Seers mated for life, seeming to never have the urge to become physical until they met the one who was right for them. She knew this, and in her attempt to remain distant and in control of herself, she had always ensured there was a certain degree of physical distance between herself and Blaez.

At this moment, however, Maelona was sure he was the right one for her because her urge to become physical with Blaez just about consumed her. It felt like every molecule of her being was begging her to let go of her tight control.

As Blaez stared down at her, she met his gaze and was pulled in by the beautiful blue depths of his eyes. Right now, they shone with desire, longing, and love.

Maelona's breaths came harsh and fast. Her heart pounded in her chest. She could feel Blaez's heart doing the same against her bare breast. He ran his hands along her back, taking his time as if he were savoring something he had desired for a long time. Finally, he dropped his mouth to hers in a searing kiss.

Maelona could feel her magic rising to the surface, swirling around them and whipping her hair to the side. Blaez's hands stroked down her back until they gripped her behind. Her magic encompassed them like a cocoon, shielding them from the outside world.

Blaez's hands moved to the back of her bare thighs. He lifted her up, and she wrapped her legs around his waist. She let out a long, low moan as she felt her most sensitive spot press against his hardness.

"You feel even better than I imagined," Blaez whispered against her mouth. Then he trailed kisses along her jawline and down her neck. Maelona dropped her head back and whispered his name.

Blaez brought his hands up and around her back and enveloped her in a tight embrace. He buried his face in the crook of her neck and breathed deeply, trying to get his physical reactions back under control. His whole body shook, even as his breathing and heart rate began to slow.

Maelona dipped her forehead to his shoulder and took some deep breaths to calm herself. Her magic slowed its spinning motion around them and slowly withdrew back inside her once again.

"I'm sorry that went so far, so fast," Blaez whispered into her ear. "I just – I want you more than words could ever express." He lifted his head just enough to lay his forehead against hers. "But our first time together is not going to be in a dank tunnel with a couple of unconscious demonkin nearby. When we are together, completely, for the first time, you will be officially mine."

Blaez let Maelona's feet touch the ground again and stepped back. He reached down to Maelona's pack and took out her clothing. He re-dressed her, one item at a time. As he worked, his fingers brushed and lingered from time to time, causing Maelona to shiver.

Once Maelona was fully dressed again, he dressed himself quickly. Maelona held her hand out to him, and he took it in his own.

"Come," she said, smiling at him lovingly, "before someone comes looking for us."

Chapter 19

As Maelona predicted, the others were waiting for them in the king's chambers when she and Blaez rejoined them a couple of hours later.

"It's about time!" Gareth exclaimed. "I was about to send out a search party."

"You sound like a worried mother hen," Maeve said to him.

"Well, better to be a worried mother hen than to wait too long and end up with dead friends," he replied.

"I can see your point," Maeve jabbed at her brother. "It took you so long to find some friends who don't get annoyed with your antics, it would be devastating to lose them so soon."

"Oh, we get annoyed with his antics," Blaez said with a grin. "but Maelona insists I not shift to my wolf and eat him."

Gareth's eyes widened at that. "Do wolves really eat human flesh?" he asked.

"Not usually," Blaez responded, quirking his brow at Gareth. "But exceptions can be made."

"Oh, lovely!" Gareth exclaimed. "It's like I now have two siblings to put up with."

Maelona smiled at them, feeling quite pleased with that comparison. It hinted that there was more of a bond forming between the two males than they liked to let on.

Maelona, Blaez, Gareth, King Niall, and Maeve sat around the large desk in the sitting area of his chambers, along with the two leaders of the Eastgate Guard, Carey, and Cathaoir.

A map spread out on the desk in front of them showed the layout for both inside and outside of the outer castle walls. King Niall, who always liked things to be direct and to the point, started by addressing Maelona. "First of all, tell us what you know," he said.

"I did not learn much new information from the demonkin," she began. "What I did learn confirmed that the dark sorcerer has been taking pains to not let anyone but his closest warriors know all his plans or all the details. The demonkin seem to believe this is because he doesn't trust anyone, or doesn't want to take the chance of the information getting out.

"I believe, and I think the other seers would agree, that he is doing this because it is a lot easier to guard just his own thoughts. It would be too difficult, even impossible, to guard the thoughts of more than himself. If he believes there are still seers alive today, or suspects there are, then he would want to lower the chances of us finding out his plans in any way that he can.

"There also seems to be a rumor circulating the lower ranks of the demonkin army that the dark sorcerer has a backup plan in case they fail to destroy the keystones. It hasn't come from official channels, though, so the demonkin I read are not sure if there is any truth to the rumors."

"Did you learn anything new about the upcoming attack on Eastgate?" King Niall asked. "Or is there anything more you know that you have not had the time to tell us before?"

"Well, as you already know," she began, "the visions we seers receive can fluctuate and change depending on a person's split-second decisions, so the future is not set in stone. Therefore, there are numerous ways the coming battle could go. At this moment, I can tell you what I foresee to be the greatest chance for success with minimal casualties. Just know that there are many players in this game. Events could always change from what we expect. So be prepared and don't take anything for granted."

She looked at each person in turn, and after they each nodded their understanding and agreement, Maelona continued by gesturing to the map once again. "I hope to keep the battle from approaching the castle walls too closely. If they get past the barbican of the outer curtain wall, the resulting chaos would make it too easy for a demonkin in disguise to slip through and sneak its way to the keep."

"I doubt they would have any more luck getting in than our guests in the dungeon had," Captain Carey said.

"That may be true," Maelona said, "but this dark sorcerer is cunning. We should not take anything for granted."

"Is their army made up mostly of demonkin?" Captain Cathaoir asked.

"Yes," Maelona replied. "But from what I have seen, the sorcerer at the root of all this likes to keep his strongest followers close, sending out his armies of Deamhain Thuaidh, the weaker demonkin, to be the fodder of the battles at the four Gates. These demonkin can project visions into the minds of humans to confuse, mislead, and torment their targets. However, since they are not fully demon, but demon-human hybrids, they need to concentrate to do this, so only the stronger and more practiced of their kind will be able to use this ability with any effectiveness during a fight.

"He has also included a small number of Deamhain Garbth Thuaidh, demonkin who can change their appearance, such as your friend the false guard, and our other three guests. They are to attempt to sneak past, undetected, while we are distracted with the battle. Their sole aim is to locate and destroy the keystone." Then turning to the king, she said, "It will be essential for you to stay close to the keystone at all time, my lord."

The king did not readily agree with Maelona. "I am the king. I should be on the front lines with my soldiers," he said in a commanding tone.

"You are the guardian of the keystone," Maelona replied in a calm but firm voice. "It is your place to be in the keep, close to the stone. You are to be our last line of defense should any slip past us."

"You are a guardian as well," Niall retorted.

"Yes, but you and I both know that my particular skills and abilities would be of better use out there," Maelona answered while gesturing outside.

The king pressed his lips together in a hard line and narrowed his eyes at Maelona. She knew he was not happy, but she also believed he knew that this was the best option.

"Let's move on," King Niall said, his eyes still narrowed in her direction.

"Maeve should be positioned at the keep with you. There is a chance that more than one demonkin may make it through."

"Wait. Wait a minute," Gareth interrupted. "Are you suggesting that my baby sister stand with my father at the keep, which is the main target for these beasts?"

"Yes, of course. Why not?" Maelona asked with a mischievous smile.

"Well, first of all, she's my baby sister…"

"I am not a child, Gareth!" Maeve interjected.

"…and second of all," Gareth continued, as if Maeve hadn't even spoken, "she has only been in combat training for a year and a half. She is not ready."

Maelona looked at Maeve and back to Gareth with a grin that said, *I know a secret.* "It is true, Gareth, that Maeve has only been training for a year and a half. However, you seem to be forgetting that, in that time, she has been training for hours upon hours, each day."

Maeve did not know how Maelona knew all of this about her, but given what her father had told her about the seers, she was not surprised.

"Also, there is one other important thing that neither you nor your sister know," Maelona continued, looking to King Niall with a conspiratorial grin. "Maeve's trainer is a seer who has lived more than seven hundred years, and he was my own trainer. His name is Donogh Carr, father to a fellow seer champion, and the best fighter the seer people have seen in a millennium."

Maeve gaped and turned to face King Niall. "Father?" she said.

"Yes, it is true," he replied. "Just before you started your training, Donogh came to me. He explained who he was and that the seers knew there was a battle coming. He insisted you needed to be prepared," he explained.

"Just for the record," he added, smiling warmly at his

daughter, "I agreed, and I am very proud of how hard you have worked and how exceptional you have become."

Maeve took her father's hand as she returned his smile with one of her own.

"And now that's out in the open, let's continue," Maelona said. "I have not been able to form a clear picture of the sorcerer who is behind all of this. But during those times when I've caught glimpses, I have gotten a strong sense of his arrogance.

"Unfortunately for us," she added, "he has reason to be arrogant. He is very powerful. Fortunately for us, however, this arrogance will cause him to greatly underestimate the resistance he will encounter at the Gates. He does not think the human protectors will be able to stand against his much stronger demonkin. He does not know that we know the nature of these demonkin, and he does not know you will have seers and shifters standing with you."

Captain Cathaoir spoke up, saying, "It is you we have to thank for this knowledge and these advantages. Most of the people here at Eastgate and the surrounding lands would have never believed this kind of alliance would be possible. We would have never believed you would stand with us after what our kind did to yours. I, personally, am grateful to you for this," he added with sincerity, "and I know our people are as well."

"What most people do not know, Captain, is that each gate is always assigned two guardians," Maelona explained. "The King of the Gate guards the keystone itself, and the second, always a seer, watches from the outside for any insidious dangers unseen to most. Therefore, it is my duty to be here for your people in times of danger."

"Well, duty or no, I thank you," Cathaoir said with a nod to her.

"As do I," agreed the king. "Is there anything else we should know?"

"Yes. Their numbers are not great as they don't expect you to have any backup. However, they do have reinforcements on the way. They will arrive after the battle begins," Maelona said.

"What kind of reinforcements?" Gareth asked suspiciously.

"Snowbeasts," Maelona replied.

The more seasoned in the group sucked in sharp breaths. Maeve and Gareth, however, who were the youngest of the group, just looked at each other in confusion.

"What is a snowbeast?" Maeve asked.

"Unpleasant," Maelona quipped.

Blaez smiled at her.

"The main thing to remember about snowbeasts," Maelona continued, "is to not stay directly in front of them for long. They have an icy breath that can freeze a man solid in moments. And from what I hear, they tend to step on their victims afterward, effectively shattering them."

"Okay. Stay away from snowbeasts," Gareth said, his mouth set in a grim line. "Noted."

After a silent pause, King Niall addressed the group with a soft voice full of unspoken concern for his family and his people. "It is late, and we will need our strength. I suggest we all turn in for the evening and begin preparations first thing in the morning."

With that, they all shuffled out of the room and to their chambers, feeling doubtful that sleep would come.

By early the next afternoon, most of the defenses were in place, and they were working on setting up the offensive weaponry. Maelona stood on the allure of the outer wall, scanning the horizon for any sign she would recognize from her visions. She had been standing there, virtually unmoving, for some time already when Blaez approached.

"The preparations seem to be going well," he commented.

"Yes," was her simple reply.

"Your brow is furrowed with worry, Maelona. Please share with me what's on your mind. Do we have no good chance of standing up against the sorcerer's army?"

"We do stand a chance of winning the day," she answered. "The trick is to successfully keep the horde from breaching the castle while minimizing casualties."

"Is that what you are worried about? Our friends being wounded, or worse?"

Maelona's gaze remained unwaveringly on the ridge in the

distance as she responded. "You know, I used to think it was a blessing that we seers cannot see our own futures, or the futures of those whose lives are, or will be, tightly entwined with our own. I always thought that it saved us from needlessly worrying, or living our lives in fear of our visions coming to pass. I believed this kind of knowledge would lead us to turn our visions into self-fulfilling prophecies.

"But now," she continued, huffing out a breath, "Now I find myself wishing I could see. The most difficult part of opening up and allowing others in is the fear of losing those you love." She paused and turned her head to look Blaez in the eye. "I fear losing *you,* mo grá."

Blaez moved behind Maelona, wrapping his arms around her as she returned her gaze forward. "You know," he said gently, his mouth close to her ear, "the seers are the only beings in the realm with this ability. I have learned from your mother that sorcerers have ways of discovering the future as well, but that what they see is not as clear. That means that the rest of us live with uncertainty of the future every moment of every day."

He brushed his lips gently along her neck before continuing. "If we always worried about what horrors await us in the future, we wouldn't be able to live our lives. We would be frozen…paralysed. Do not let your worries paralyze you, Maelona. Trust that I can take care of myself."

Blaez stayed behind Maelona as she stood quietly contemplating his words. He stayed there with her while the hours passed and she stood watch. He kept his arms wrapped around her, hoping she could feel his warmth and support.

Chapter 20

It was late afternoon when Maelona finally spotted the movement she'd been waiting for, just over the ridge in the distance. "It's time," she said quietly, and Blaez threw his head back and let out a howl as a sign to the others.

As Maelona and Blaez descended from the allure, they were met at the foot of the steps by Gareth and King Niall.

"So, I see you can do more than growl like a wolf in your human form," Gareth said. "That was a pretty impressive howl. I made a sound like that once, when a horse accidentally kicked me in the..."

"Okay, we get it," Blaez interrupted. "Do you not realize we are about to go into battle? Are you never serious?"

"I try not to be," Gareth answered.

Maelona shook her head at the two males.

The residents of the town of Eastgate who had fled to safety at the castle had been relocated to the inner bailey in anticipation of today's battle. Now, King Niall turned to address his soldiers, who had gathered in the outer bailey. "Remember what you have been taught," he began. "Our enemies are not humans, but demonkin. They are large and strong, but we are quick and smart - and we have right on our side. Keep yourselves moving, especially when the snowbeasts arrive. Do not make yourselves targets. Stay calm and steady; do not let them into your heads. Believe what you know to be true. Also, do not lose heart when the beasts come. Remember, once the enemy shows its hand, our backup will arrive."

A dozen archers ran by and up to the allure as Maelona, Blaez, and Gareth moved forward to join the two dozen men and women that made up the king's guard and soldiers. Another two dozen local men and women took position inside the gate of the outer bailey, ready to fight off any demonkin who might make it through. As soon as King Niall was satisfied that everyone was in place, he headed back to the keep, where Maeve was already in position, to stand guard with her.

Gareth, Maelona, and captains Carey and Cathaoir positioned the men in ranks a few hundred meters from the castle gate. Soon, the enemy forces became visible over the ridge, heading toward them at a steady rate. The Eastgate ranks held their place unwaveringly, hoping to draw the enemy within range of the archers. As if they understood what they were thinking, the demonkin stopped just out of range.

After a short stand-off, Maelona decided to try to goad them into attacking first. Through her visions, she had learned many things about the demonkin. She knew that females were not looked upon with high regard in demonkin society, so she figured it had to irk the demonkin who seemed to be the leader that he was facing a female right now. The way he glared at her seemed to support this theory.

Also through her dream-visions, Maelona had learned a demonkin insult or two. Knowing that demonkin also tended to be impetuous and easily angered, she rotated her sword in her hand, then brought it in an arc above her head before slicing it diagonally through the air in front of her. She held the demonkin captain's gaze and gave him a mocking smile as she did so.

This was a quite blatant threat amongst demonkin, and the demonkin captain was receiving it from a female no less! Raising his sword in the air, he roared with rage and charged forward, his troops following on his heels.

The army of Eastgate stood firm as the demonkin came barrelling toward them. Once they were in range of the archers, Maelona raised her hand in the air. The row of foot soldiers kneeled with their shields lifted diagonally, bottoms touching the earth at their feet and tops tilted over their heads to protect them. Then, she brought her arm forward, and the archers let loose a volley of arrows from the top of the outer wall.

The demonkin had a line of archers as well and let loose a volley of their own. The Eastgate soldiers were protected by their shield formation, so there was little in the way of damage to them.

Demonkin dropped all around their captain, and yet he charged toward Maelona with a single-minded focus. After the arrows had passed overhead, the few soldiers with mounts who were lined up at the back took off, jumping over the line of soldiers crouched at the front and galloping toward the enemy with sword and pike at the ready. As soon as the horses were clear, the crouching soldiers stood and ran forward to meet the demonkin army.

Maelona let out a wordless, yet menacing, battle cry as she began charging forward to meet the demonkin captain. Maelona wanted to keep it off balance, sensing that this beast was a real danger, so she ducked in and out amongst the enemy, taunting him with her presence and taking down the closest enemy before disappearing again.

Maelona was a force to be reckoned with as she took down a demonkin, then launched herself over it to take on the next enemy to get in her way.

Maelona made sure to always be aware of where Blaez was, glancing over at him from time to time. He was a sight to behold. He would attack in wolf form, take down his target, change to human form as he leaped, roll to his feet, and grab a weapon as he did so. Maelona was glad to see that he took what she had taught him to heart with such exuberance.

Maelona noticed also noticed that Donogh Carr and Maeve fought side by side some distance away, cutting through the demonkin that set upon them in waves.

At one point, Maelona and Blaez kept eye contact for too long. A demonkin rushed up behind him. He turned to the sound, but he didn't even have time to position himself to defend.

Maelona grabbed a throwing knife from a holder on her chest strap and threw it with amazing force and accuracy. The blade whizzed past Blaez's ear and planted itself right between the demonkin's eyes. Blaez turned back to look at her, and she nodded to him before she turned to face another enemy.

Maelona tried to scan the periphery as often as she could. After a time, she noticed huge, lumbering forms heading toward them from the direction of the ridge. She yelled, "Brace yourselves! The beasts are coming."

The people of Eastgate paused for just a second as three very large beasts with matted white fur, dulled by the elements, came ambling over the ridge. They looked like huge hyenas, dog-like in form. Longer legs in front than in back made them taller at the shoulder than at the rump. They were twice as tall as a human man, and they came charging into the fray.

"Smelly dragon turds!" Gareth suddenly exclaimed from just behind Maelona's right shoulder. "What are those?"

"Smelly dragon turds?" Maelona asked, looking at him with her brow raised. "Did you just make that up?"

"Yes."

"Did you just blurt out the most ridiculous thing you could think of off the top of your head?"

"Maybe. Now back to my original question. What *are* those things? They're humongous!"

"Those, my friend, are the snowbeasts I told you about," Maelona replied with a sinister smile. "And the earth will shake when they hit the ground." She spun her sword in her hand as she spoke.

"You really do enjoy fighting a little too much, don't you?" Gareth gave her a sideways glance, looking at her as if she were crazy.

But Maelona was no longer paying attention to him. "Move!" she bellowed, and she started to run forward to aid an Eastgate soldier who was now in range of the beast's ice breath. Without pausing in her run, Maelona whipped out a throwing knife, driving it with force and accuracy into the side of the beast's neck. This did not slow the beast down, but its attention shifted off its intended target. It whipped its head in her direction, freezing any vegetation in its path.

Maelona swung her head left, then right, taking in the battle all around her. The soldiers of Eastgate were holding their own, as were Blaez, Carasek, and the shifter protectors who had run into the fray once the snowbeasts had arrived. However, the snowbeasts were almost upon them. She knew they would not refrain from destroying her people even if there were demonkin among them.

Fortunately, some shifters were now close enough to hear Maelona as she called to them. "Carasek! Aengus! Caer!" she yelled, knowing who was who even in their wolf forms. When they looked in her direction, she continued, "Get them to open their mouths."

The wolves nodded their heads and went running toward the snowbeasts. *Fire! I need fire!* Maelona thought frantically, looking all around her as she ran. *If only it were night time and torches were lit.* Then, suddenly, she could feel a prickling of electricity under her skin, and she remembered what her mother had said to her about embracing who she is.

She let go of her control completely, thinking, *I don't need fire, I am fire!* With this thought, her skin heated to such an intense degree that an approaching demonkin jolted back at the feel of it. Then, holding out her hand, palm up, Maelona focused some energy into the shape and size of a large stone. Only, instead of stone, it was made of pure fire.

She turned to track where Carasek and Aengus were and spotted Aengus' wolf approaching the closest snowbeast from the rear. He jumped up and latched his teeth onto the tendon of the beast's hind leg. The beast then did two things at once: it flicked back the paw Aengus was attached to, sending him flying, and it opened its mouth in a roar of pain.

Maelona quickly took advantage of this opening and threw her hand forward with great force and velocity. Her aim was true, and her fireball went straight into the beast's open maw. The snowbeast closed its mouth, its throat working as if it were swallowing. It let out another roar of pain. The earth shuddered as it fell to the ground. It shook violently for a few moments, then stilled in death.

Once she was satisfied that it was dead, Maelona looked for

Aengus to ensure he was okay. However, she had only gone a few steps before she whipped around to face the second beast that was now charging her. It had already opened its mouth to breathe its ice breath in her direction, and so she had no time to think; she could only react. Her instincts took over, and she held up her hands in front of her, palms out, sending white-hot flames to meet the snowbeast's breath. She watched as the flames hit the ice only a couple of feet in front of her.

Channels of electricity suddenly seemed to flow up through the ice and toward the beast as well. This electrical energy charged out in front of the fire. The fire then chased the electricity up the icy path created by the beast's breath until they both traveled inside the beast's body. However, the beast did not just shudder and fall to the ground dead as the other one had. This time, when the electricity and fire entered the snowbeast's body, it exploded into the air, many pieces of its flesh obliterating into ash as the beast's fragments fell back to the ground.

Chapter 21

Over near the barbican, a group of Eastgate soldiers guarded the gate against any enemy who might try to get through. Gareth had come to lend his support when he saw a group of demonkin charging that way. Now, he engaged a stone-colored demonkin.

One of his Eastgate soldiers, Keena, even closer to the portcullis than he was, was engaged with both a stone-colored demonkin and a mottled-red colored demonkin. Gareth knew what this color difference signified, thanks to the information that Maelona had given them. He knew he needed to get over to Keena to help her. However, he had to take care of his own opponent before he could do that.

He fought sword to sword against his foe. The demonkin was lumbering and a little clumsy, but it was strong. Gareth knew from experience that if he let even one blow touch him, it could spell disaster. He deflected a blow by bringing his sword across to strike from the outside. He continued to push his opponent's sword across the front of its body until the demonkin was off balance. As the demonkin stumbled, it bent forward, allowing Gareth to see another demonkin running toward him.

Gareth swept his sword along the back of the thighs of the demonkin in front of him, effectively hamstringing him. When this first demonkin dropped to its knees, Gareth leaped onto its back and jumped into the air. He raised his sword above his head, blade pointed down, intending to skewer his new opponent swiftly so he could get to Keena. The demonkin reacted by aiming its sword up toward Gareth, who could do nothing but twist his now-airborne body to try to avoid his enemy's blade.

Gareth managed to avoid being run through himself, but only just. The demonkin's blade grazed his side, but Gareth managed to keep his focus through the sudden pain. Though his strike wasn't as true as intended, he still managed to drive his blade down through the side of his enemy's neck. As his own body hit the ground, so did the now lifeless body of his opponent.

The breath had been knocked from Gareth's body when it impacted the ground. He hardly had time to catch his breath again, however, when he noticed that his first, now crippled opponent had managed to grab a pike from a nearby corpse. The demonkin was trying to position its now uncooperative body so he could run Gareth through. Before it could, however, Gareth grabbed a dagger from his boot and threw it full-force at the demonkin, hitting it in the throat. The demonkin made disgusting gurgling noises until it finally lay still.

Gareth pulled himself up from the ground and looked over to where Keena had been standing. Her body now lay on the ground, along with the body of the gray demonkin. The mottled-red skinned demonkin was standing over Keena's body, pulling its blade from her chest. Gareth's own chest twisted and constricted with pain at the sight. He was too late. *I've failed her,* he thought.

Gareth was not given time to dwell on his sorrow, for as he watched, steam or smoke of some sort seemed to rise off the demonkin's body. As the smoke got thicker, it wrapped around the demonkin's form. It changed color and solidified until Gareth was now looking at Keena's likeness. The demonkin then walked toward the barbican with a purposeful stride.

Gareth suddenly felt white-hot rage rise inside of him. This beast who had just killed Keena, his father's loyal soldier, now dared to wear her likeness! He looked around himself for a weapon he could use. A couple of feet to his left, he spotted a demonkin corpse holding a bow. Gareth hurried to the body, grabbed the bow and an arrow from the nearby quiver. He nocked the arrow, drew it back, and aimed. Then he yelled,

"Hey, ugly!" and let the arrow fly.

The demonkin, disguised as Keena, paused mid-stride and turned its head in Gareth's direction when it heard Gareth's yell. Gareth watched as his arrow hit its mark, piercing the demonkin's left eye. The demonkin, still looking at Gareth, took a couple of steps forward. Then, its illusion flickered and died just before it dropped to the ground dead.

Gareth lowered his hands to his sides and stood for a moment in disbelief. He looked around himself at the three opponents he just took down.

Oh…my…I can't believe I did that! Gareth thought. He was considered an expert marksman in archery and knife-throwing in the training field, but he never had to use these skills in battle before today. He would have never thought that practice on a target, as extensive as his father had ensured it was, could translate to the stress of a battlefield. As he had gotten better and better in practice, he had started working with moving targets. Sometimes he would be on horseback, targeting stationary objects. Sometimes the targets were mounted on horses. Sometimes, both himself and his target would be mounted.

Still, as skilled as he had become, he had been told time and again that real battle would be nothing like targeting inanimate objects. And really, it was not. He didn't know if it was skill or luck, but either way, he was grateful for his victories – for surviving - today. Suddenly he wondered if Maelona had put a protection spell on his amulet after all.

The area he stood in was now relatively quiet. Gareth shook himself from his reverie and turned to try to locate his friends. He turned just in time to see a snowbeast explode and incinerate right before his eyes. Maelona was standing not far from this scene, and now she was scanning the area, looking for something.

Gareth's eyes traveled across the landscape to the right of her. Suddenly, his eyes stopped on Blaez, who was surrounded by demonkin, Gareth noticed a demonkin creep up behind Blaez as he was distracted by the others. Seeing what the demonkin intended to do, Gareth took off in their direction, yelling to both Blaez and Maelona as he went. They were far enough away that, with the sounds of battle going on between their positions, he doubted they could hear them. But he had to try.

Before the smoke had even cleared from the exploding snowbeast, Maelona searched the scene again for the other one. Before she could locate it, however, the smoke did clear, and she saw a sight she had been praying would not come to pass. It was not a dream-vision that she had received herself. No, she was too close to Blaez for that. Rather, it was information that had been passed along to her from Talwyn, her fellow seer champion, the last time she had Blaez guard her while she slept in the woods.

Blaez was engaged in a fight in human form, blocking blows from a demonkin's sword. While he focused on defending the onslaught from two demonkin, yet another figure moved up behind him. She now realized it was the demonkin captain who had glared at Maelona across the field at the start of the battle.

Too far away to reach him in time, Maelona could do nothing but watch as the captain's blade pierced Blaez's back and jutted out through his abdomen.

Before the demonkin even had time to remove his blade, Maelona was on top of him. He barely had time to raise his shield before she started pummelling him with the hilt of her sword. She continued strike, after strike, after strike, her sword upon his shield, until it cracked and he finally fell to the ground, dropping the broken shield in front of him.

At one point, the two other demonkin attempted to come to their captain's aid. But Maelona was so enraged that her power was radiating from her body. When the demonkin approached within a few feet of her, they screamed in agony before slowly dissolving into dust. After that, no one else dared approach her.

Maelona flipped the captain over to lie on its back, then straddled its body, continuing her assault bare-handed until the demonkin was a bruised and bloodied mess laying in the dirt. But she did not kill it. No. She had a better use for it.

Grabbing her sword and standing back up, she pointed her

sword at its throat. "Get up," she growled in a low and menacing voice. "GET UP!" she repeated, screaming the words at him this time.

The demonkin captain slowly and unsteadily climbed back to its feet and stood there, swaying in front of her, barely holding onto consciousness.

Maelona moved in front of it until they were almost nose to nose, wanting to ensure that it heard and understood what she had to say. Her body trembled with the force of her barely-controlled anger, but her voice was strong and steady as she spoke.

"You go back to your *emperor*," she spat. "You go back, and you tell him that we will *never* give in! You tell him that we would rather die here today, standing against him, then live lifetimes kneeling at his feet!" In a low, menacing voice, she added, "You tell him that we are coming for him."

Acting on instinct rather than conscious thought, she looked around until she spotted the last snowbeast.

"Beast, come here!" she yelled, her voice carrying across the field.

Everyone, ally and enemy alike, paused in their fighting, looking on in awe as the beast stopped mid-attack and did as she commanded. It was compelled to do so by her magic, which she was now using instinctually.

When the snowbeast reached her side, it crouched down next to her. Then she grabbed the demonkin captain, who was too weak and battered to protest, and threw it up onto the beast's back.

"Rope!" she yelled, and an Eastgate soldier standing close to her took a coil he had attached at his waist and handed it to her.

She roughly secured the demonkin to the snowbeast with the rope so it would not fall off along the way. Then in a firm and commanding voice, she said to the snowbeast, "Go to your master." Without hesitation, it ran off the way it had come, and when it once again reached the ridge, Maelona turned and ran to Blaez.

Gareth was already there tending to him, and, upon her approach, he looked up to meet her gaze. With watery eyes and sorrow clear on his face, he shook his head at her.

Maelona dropped to her knees next to Blaez. She felt as though she could hardly breathe through the agony that constricted her chest. She could not bear the thought of living her life without him.

Throwing back her head, she screamed wordlessly. The force of her sorrow and anguish was so strong that her magic exploded out from her body in a shockwave.

But this time, it was not like what had happened with her father and Blyth Murdax. This time, she could feel every single life force her magic touched. She could feel the light and the dark. And as her power surged outwards, she left all the light standing and obliterated all the dark.

Then, suddenly, her power was sucked back into her in a rush as she felt something surprising and unexpected.

She felt…hope. She felt a tiny flicker of life where she had thought there was none.

"He is still alive," she whispered. Then, louder, "He is still alive!" And she knew what she had to do.

She knew he was close to passing back into the universe, and she didn't have much time. She needed to expose him inside and out. She placed one hand under Blaez's neck at the base of his skull and lifted, tilting his head until his mouth and throat opened. Moving her hand to his forehead, she placed her other hand on the wound on his chest and leaned down, covering his mouth with her own.

Gareth was still on the other side of Blaez, and he had watched on as sorrow and devastation had washed over Maelona's features. He had felt her anguish as her magic passed through him. Yet now she emanated hope.

At first, as Maelona leaned down and put her lips on Blaez, he thought she was kissing him in a last farewell of sorts. He noticed a pale lavender glow coming from underneath Maelona's hand, then from around their joined mouths, and he realized what she was doing.

With the hand that was touching his wound, Maelona attempted to heal Blaez's external wound while at the same time tried to heal him from the inside by breathing her magic into him. Gareth was amazed when he noticed Blaez's eyelids flutter. Then, after a couple of moments, Blaez opened his eyes and breathed the name, "Maelona."

Maelona looked down into Blaez's loving gaze, and she burst into tears of joy and relief. She leaned down to give him another gentle kiss before she dropped her head to his chest and quietly sobbed.

Gareth looked at his friends with compassion, joy, and amazement. Even though he understood what had happened and that there was magic involved, he couldn't help but feel that he had just witnessed the impossible, and he was awed. Above all else, he was grateful for fate bringing these two beings into his life.

When he first met Maelona, and as he had gotten to know her, he had hoped there could be more between them. Yet, he was not disappointed at how things turned out. He saw what Maelona and Blaez had, what Maelona and his own father had, and he understood the difference. He hoped they would all remain lifelong friends, as Maelona and his father had.

Once Maelona had calmed considerably, Gareth stood and offered her his hand. "Come, Maelona," he said. "Let's go find our friend here a nice room with a soft bed and start a fire for him." Maelona reached up to take his hand, giving him a grateful smile. As she stood, Gareth glanced up, and then he froze.

All around them, over the complete field of battle, every last one of the demonkin was gone. Only scorched, black earth remained to mark where they once had stood. Yet most of their allies were still standing.

"Umm, maybe you should have done that at the *beginning* of the battle." Gareth quipped.

"I didn't know I *could* do that at the beginning of the battle," Maelona returned with a sad smile, suddenly sounding exhausted.

Chapter 22

Blaez awoke slowly, looking up at the stone ceiling of his room in the castle. Looking around in the light of day, he could see that it was a nicely appointed room with wall tapestries and a hearth where a low fire now burned. Judging by the light that filtered in through the window, he guessed it was around midday.

He was surprised to find himself alone. He had awoken in the dark of night, only to find Maelona sleeping next to him, clinging to him like she would never let go. The memory warmed him inside and made him smile.

Just then, he heard the door creak open and turned to see Maelona entering, carrying a tray of food.

Seeing that he was awake, she smiled at him warmly and said, "I brought you some lunch. You need to keep up your strength, so you can fully recuperate."

"Thank you, mo grá," Blaez said, sitting up slowly and carefully and taking the tray from her.

"I'm sorry I had to leave you this morning," she said, moving to sit on the bed beside him. "I had to check on things."

"Will you give me the update?" he asked.

"Well," she began slowly, "when I thought you were –," she paused to swallow back her emotion. "When I thought the demonkin captain had killed you," she said, shuddering as she remembered, "my magic responded similarly to the way it had at the Crater of Sorrows. Except, this time, I could distinguish the dark souls from the light, and only the dark ones were destroyed. All the demonkin were destroyed, save one."

She paused a moment before continuing. "I remember what happened, and what I felt. If it was passed over, that could only mean there is more light in it than darkness."

"Is that possible?" Blaez queried, surprise evident in his voice.

"Do you remember what my mother said about how there are always exceptions, how there are always those who defy the nature of their kind?"

"I do," Blaez replied, nodding.

"Well, it would seem we have found one of those exceptions," she explained with a small smile. "The King's Guard insisted on placing it in the dungeon until we know for sure where it stands. I am going to speak with it a little later."

"I'm going with you," Blaez stated.

"Oh no, you are not!" Maelona replied. "I was able to repair some of the damage with my magic, but not all. You still need to rest and recover."

"You are not going to go talk to a demonkin alone are you?"

"He is imprisoned. Chained to the wall. The guards are not taking any chances. However, I will take Gareth with me if it will help you relax some."

"Thank you," Blaez said. Maelona smiled and leaned forward to place a gentle kiss on his lips.

"What other news?" Blaez prompted.

"Aengus was injured when a snowbeast threw him. He was stunned momentarily, and while he was down, a demonkin approached him with its sword raised, intending to finish him…"

"No!" Blaez breathed, anticipating what she would say next.

But Maelona shook her head as she continued, "Aengus was not killed. Breoc saved him."

"Breoc?"

"Yes," she nodded, but her expression was solemn, and he dreaded to hear what she would say next.

"When Breoc saw what was happening, that Aengus was

down and in danger of being killed, he charged at the demonkin. The demonkin was startled, and turned toward Breoc with its weapon raised." There was a quiver in her voice when she added, "It struck him straight through the heart."

"No! Breoc…he was so young!"

"He was a hero, Blaez," Maelona replied. Her voice was low but firm. "Yes, the demonkin sealed Breoc's fate, but Breoc ripped its throat out on his way down. Breoc fell as a hero, Blaez. He saved Aengus' life."

Blaez took a few moments to allow himself to quietly grieve. Then he took a deep breath, calming himself before he sent up a silent prayer for the safe passage of the young protector's soul.

"Who else?" he asked.

"Renny was seriously injured," she said, referring to the young, female protector. "She was brought to one of Eastgate's healers. Gareth gave them some leighis leaf and explained to them how to use it."

Blaez raised his eyebrows at this. "I guess he's been paying attention," he said.

"It would seem so," Maelona agreed with a smile. Then she continued, "She is already almost completely healed.

"The king lost three of his soldiers, and Cathaoir was also seriously injured. He was treated by the healers and is doing much better now."

"I am glad to hear he will be okay."

"There were numerous other injuries as well," she added, "but nothing else serious. Overall, we were very lucky."

Blaez took Maelona by the hands, then dipped his head to encourage her to meet his gaze. "And how about you, mo grá? How are you feeling? I know that you hate to take lives…"

"It's true," she interrupted, "that I hate to take life unnecessarily. But in this case," she added with sadness in her voice, "I felt their life forces before they died. There was no remorse in them and, for most of them, if they had lived, they might have gone on to kill many innocent people."

"I'm guessing," Blaez said as he stroked the back of her hands soothingly with his thumbs, "that you are having some trouble coming to terms with all this death anyway."

With a small, sad smile, she responded, "You know me well. I hate knowing that I am capable of such destruction. No one being should hold that kind of power."

Before Blaez had a chance to respond to that – to remind her she was capable of great healing as well; to remind her that the universe gifted her with this power for a reason – she changed the subject.

"There is one more thing, but I am not yet sure what to make of it," she went on uncertainly. "It was Gareth who went deep into the keep to inform Maeve and the king that the battle was over. They apparently had not seen any sign of demonkin or any other sort of trouble while they were down there during the battle."

"Well, that is a positive thing, is it not?" Blaez inquired.

"Yes, of course it is," Maelona agreed. "But this morning I awoke early to this nagging sense of worry. I could not shake the feeling that something was wrong. So, I went down to the keep to check on the keystone," she explained. "When I placed my hand on the stone, I was flooded with feelings: fear, anger, pain. At the same time, I was hit with many random, disjointed images, and I am sure none of these were my own."

"Okay," Blaez said slowly, carefully considering her words. "That adds another, unknown complication to the mix. So, we hope that the other seers were successful in guarding their keystones, as we were here. However, we continue with the plan we discussed with your mother and the elders. We march on to the Great Gate, meeting the other seers and shifters there as planned. And we also plan for the possibility that the sorcerer behind all of this and all his evil followers will be waiting for us when we arrive with some cruel plan."

Maelona simply nodded her agreement before adding, "That is really our only choice."

She and Blaez remained lost in thought for a few more moments before Maelona spoke again.

"There will be a ceremony on the field of battle tonight at dusk to honor the fallen," she said. "Do you feel strong enough to attend?"

"I would come even if I had to crawl there," Blaez responded. "However, thanks to you, that won't be necessary. I am feeling much better than I should, considering I was almost dead yesterday afternoon." He smiled warmly at Maelona and squeezed her hands gently.

Maelona looked down at their entwined hands. In a quiet voice, with just a bit of a waver, she admitted, "I was so scared Blaez. I thought I had lost you."

"I am here, mo grá. Thanks to you. And I promise to do my best to be here for you for as long as the universe allows."

Maelona simply nodded again, her emotions making her throat too tight to speak. Then she took a deep breath and looked up to meet his gaze, just before leaning forward to touch her lips to his.

As the sun dipped below the horizon that evening, all the wolf shifter protectors who had aided at the Battle of Eastgate joined with the humans. They gathered together on the field in front of the castle, where pyres had been built for Breoc and the three fallen soldiers of Eastgate. Maelona, Blaez, Carasek, Gareth, Maeve, King Niall, and Carey had positioned themselves around the pyres with lit torches in their hands.

Handing her torch to Blaez, Maelona moved in front of the pyres, raising her hands in the air and her eyes skyward. Then she began to sing an ancient seer prayer-song that was still sung to this day for departed loved ones. No other in the group understood the ancient language, yet they all felt the sentiment of love, loss, and giving oneself over to the universe as the beautiful melody flowed through them.

Next, Caellum, as first in command of the protectors, began to sing a shifter prayer-song. The other shifters present, including Maelona, joined in as he sang:

> Every evening as the moon shines bright,
> Breaking its way through the dark of the night,
> We will sound our sorrow and remembrance.
>
> Each morning as the sun rises high,
> Bringing its warmth and its light to the sky,
> We remember, the universe holds your essence.
>
> We are not alone; your spirit is always near,
> Touching us all as we remain here:
> We, your people, celebrate your transcendence.

Following the prayer-songs, the people stood in complete silence, showing their respect to their departed loved-ones. After this period of silence, the king turned to address all who were present.

"Since our customs state that once the pyres are lit, we spend the next day in silence in reverent memory of our fallen, I wish to say my piece now, so that you all have time to think on what I have to say, and to prepare, if necessary.

"Friends and family," he began, gesturing around him. "brave Breoc of the wolf shifters, and valiant Varden, Keena, and Brieg of Eastgate all believed that our freedom was important enough to fight for. To die for. They understood that by failing to act now, we increase the chance of losing our future and our freedom to the forces who wish to subjugate us.

"With all their hearts and souls, they believed in the righteousness and justice of our cause. They were determined to not stand by and become victims. They chose instead to be heroes, doing whatever they had in their power to do, to stand against our foes.

"Do not doubt for a moment, my people, that the battle we

saw here was only the beginning. We have won the day, but the largest battle is yet to be fought. Will we remain here at Eastgate, letting others fight a war that will ultimately decide the fate of our world and all who live in it? I think not.

"Maelona Sima, the wolf shifter protectors here in our presence today, and my own son and daughter will be leaving Eastgate a few days from now to march toward the Great Gate. They will be met there by numerous other seers, many shifters of various species, and human warriors from the other gate towns and beyond. I must stay here with a number of my Royal Guard to keep watch over our keystone. It is my purpose and my responsibility to do so, even as I long to be with you on the fields of battle.

"I ask that every soldier willing to fight - everyone who values our world and our way of life - meet in the outer bailey at sunrise the day after tomorrow, once our Day of Silence is over. I ask that you plan and prepare for the coming fight. I ask that you march to the Great Gate with the intention of winning the day, and thereby securing our freedom and our future.

"I ask you, my people, to fight valiantly, with all your hearts and souls, never once allowing yourself to forget what is on the line."

Pausing in his speech to turn and look at the pyres, he added, "I ask you, my friends, to fight as Breoc, Varden, Keena, and Brieg have done. We cannot let their sacrifices be in vain. We CANNOT let the darkness swallow the light!"

With this last, he touched his torch to the nearest pyre, and his fellow torch-holders did the same. All the people stood watch as the bodies of their friends turned to ash and were carried on the wind back into the universe.

Chapter 23

Blaez rested before the fire around suppertime the night before they were slated to head out for the Great Gate. Deep in thought, he watched the embers flicker in the fire. He was so engrossed that he almost didn't hear the door as Maelona entered.

He turned and watched her place a tray on the table next to the bed before coming over to stand close to him by the fireside.

Before she had a chance to speak, however, Blaez looked up at her, catching her gaze as he stood.

"Why must it be you to carry the Ternias to the Great Gate?" he blurted out. "Is there no one else who could take on that task? Carrying it will make you a target for the sorcerer."

"And who else would you have take my place, Blaez?" she asked softly, patiently. "What other life would I place below my own?"

"Mine!" he answered vehemently. "I will carry it for you! I just – I cannot bear the thought of anything happening to you."

Maelona smiled sadly at Blaez before taking him by the hand. "Come," she said, and she led him over to the tray she had brought in.

It took Blaez a moment to recognize the items he saw before him, and when he did, it triggered a flood of memories from childhood.

From a very young age, every wolf shifter in his village was tasked with creating a mark, a symbol that would represent them. For most young ones, there was much trial and error and many revisions before they finally created a mark that they felt truly represented themselves.

They practiced making their mark, over and over again, until they got it just right. They used animal skins to practice placing their marks on, using items such as the ones Maelona had laid out on the tray. There were several small bowls with different dyes made from plants and insects, a couple of hollow needles made of metal or bone, and a very strong and pure alcohol to clean the needles with.

Sometimes shifters used their marks as a kind of signature. Sometimes they scratched it on stones or in the bark of trees to mark territory or to announce that they had passed by. But the main reason wolf-shifter young were taught how to do this and made to practice it until it was just right, was because they would one day place this mark upon a chosen mate. It was a sign of their love and respect for one another, and of the partnership they were entering into for life.

Blaez's eyes jumped back up to Maelona and, for the first time since she had entered the room, he noticed her clothing. Instead of wearing the practical leather clothing of a warrior that he was used to seeing her in, she now wore a long flowing green robe, which he recognized to be the robe of a mating ceremony. He had never actually seen one before, as shifter mating ceremonies were always just between the mating pair, but as with the mark, they were all taught about them as children.

He looked into Maelona's eyes, his gaze searching her own.

"Before you say anything or give your answer," she said, "I have some things to say, and something important to tell you."

"Go on," he prompted. It was hard for him to remain calm. This was everything he had been dreaming of. However, he was also a little apprehensive. He wanted to make sure she was certain of her decision and ready for it.

"As I am sure you could tell," she began, "I was drawn to you from the very start. I have never before felt the desire to open up to someone so quickly. It soon became clear to me that I was not going to be able to hold you at a distance, as I do with everyone else. I tried hard, though, because I knew the nature of the threat coming our way and I feared for the future. What would it mean, for example, if I failed to learn to control my power? How would I feel if I let you in and something happened to you, or if I were to accidentally hurt you? Would it make me lose control if it did? And, most importantly how would *you* feel if something were to happen to me?"

Blaez opened his mouth to respond, but Maelona held up her hand to stop him, saying, "Please, let me finish everything I have to say first. It could make a difference.

"Even after I realized that I was fighting a losing battle by trying to keep some distance between us," she continued, "I feared giving in completely, because of the things I know and what they could mean for my future. But after almost losing you," she said, swallowing back emotion, "I realized something.

"I realized," she went on, "that none of us know for certain what the future will bring. And as you have pointed out to me, we can't let our fears keep us from living in the present. In that moment, when I thought you were gone to me forever, I was in anguish! I mourned the time and the closeness I lost with you because of my worries and fears. And then when I realized you were still living, I vowed to myself that I would open up to you and place my feelings fully before you. I vowed that I would tell you the one thing that makes me most worry for you if we are to be together. I vowed that I would put it all out there and then let you decide."

"Please Maelona," Blaez begged, "please tell me what this thing is that you think would make me turn away from my feelings for you."

Maelona looked down at her feet and swallowed nervously. Then she took a deep breath, gathered her courage, and lifted her head up to look Blaez in the eyes.

"The reason why no one else can be given my task, Blaez - the reason why it must be me - is that I am…" Maelona hesitated for a moment before continuing. "I am *fated* for this, Blaez. The sorceress Scota, who foresaw what is happening right now, who foresaw the Ternias – she foresaw my birth. She foresaw my role in this part of our history. I worry about our future together because I know I am meant to stop the evil forces at the Great Gate, but I do not know if I am meant to survive it."

Blaez froze for a few moments as he let the shock of this new information sink in. He eventually became aware that Maelona had stopped talking and was looking at him expectantly, anxiously awaiting his response.

Grabbing both of Maelona's hands, he said, "Since we do not know how much time we have, which I still say we never really knew anyway, let's not waste one more moment of it."

With that, he removed his vest and moved to the bed, where he propped up some pillows so he could sit semi-reclined against the wall.

Maelona pulled the table close to the bed so she could reach what she needed as she worked, then she climbed onto the bed and kneeled, straddling his thighs with her own. She worked slowly and painstakingly, taking her time as she lovingly placed her mark on the left side of his chest, close to his heart.

When she was done, Blaez picked her up and turned her over so that he was now above her, lowering the top of her robe enough to work. Just as Maelona had done, he took his time as he carefully placed his mark on her, leaving him with an overwhelming sense of joy and pride once it was complete.

Then, Maelona gently pushed Blaez up and back as she rose to her knees to face him on the bed. Their bodies pressed close together, leaving only enough space between them for her to place her hand over her mark on his chest, and he on hers, before then reciting the simple words that were customary for a wolf shifter mating.

"I am yours," Maelona said,

"And I am yours," Blaez returned.

And then, just a breath before their lips came together in a passionate, loving kiss filled with promises of things to come, they recited the final words together.

"We shall never be alone."

I wake up from dreams
Of dark and light,
Of endless skies
On a star-filled night.
Of goodness that shines through
When all hope seems lost,
Though our victories be won
At the dearest cost.
When fires light the night
And the battle sounds,
When everything quakes,
From the trees to the ground,
Remember those
We are fighting for:
The old, the young,
The innocent, the poor.
Take courage from our friends,
Instill fear in our foes,
We will gather a strength
Such as no other knows.
I wake up from dreams
Of sorrow and fear.
When our enemies fall
Will we still be here?

Glossary of Terminology

Anceannmor: An evil and powerful sorcerer who discovered how to use the power at the hub of the ley lines to create a magical gate that would allow demons from another realm to pass over into the realm of Sterrenvar

Anum cara: Soul friend

Axes: Points where two ley lines join, resulting in increased magical power

Cruache Mountains: A mountain range to the south of the Foraoise Naofa and outside of the magical ley lines

Daine Garbth Thuaidh: A race of humans who live in the northern regions of Sterrenvar; generally stouter and rougher than the Daine Thuaidh

Daine Thuaidh: A race of humans who live in the northern regions of the realm of Sterrenvar

Deamhain Garbth Thuaidh: Demonkin who are the result of breeding between the original demons brought over by Anceannmor and the human race, Daine Garbth Thuaidh. Anceannmor purposefully bred a species of demon that was known for possessing human bodies with the Daine Garbth Thuaidh. The resulting demonkin could not possess bodies, but could change their outward appearance by means of illusion to impersonate humans.

Deamhain Thuaidh: Demonkin who are the result of breeding between the original demons brought over by Anceannmor and the human race, Daine Thuaidh. The resulting demonkin could project images into the minds of humans in order to mislead and torment them.

Demonkin: Descendants of demons that bred with humans who lived to the north of the realm

Demons: Evil beings originally from another realm that were brought through the Great Gate by Anceannmor to help form his army and subjugate the land

Dream-visions: True visions of the past or present, and true or possible visions of the future that the seers receive as they sleep when their minds are most open to the messages of the universe

Foraoise Naofa: Also known as the Sacred Forest. A dense forest range found within the magical ley lines at the center of the realm of Sterrenvar, and home to most of the magical races of Sterrenvar.

Galanite: A very strong and light metal found beneath the Cruache Mountains; very useful for fabricating armor and weaponry

Gates: Eastgate, Westgate, Southgate, Northgate were fortresses built atop the keystones to protect them. They eventually developed into castle towns.

Great Gate: The gate formed from magically imbued, large, rectangular, and upright stones placed in a circular pattern (similar to Stonehenge) on top of the hub of the ley lines. This gate stabilizes the power at the hub, allowing a portal to be opened between realms. Anceannmor created the Great Gate with the intention of freeing demons to cross over and form his army, which he would then use to subjugate the realm of Sterrenvar and all its people.

Guardians: Those assigned the responsibility of protecting the realm and/or the keystones

Hub: The center of the diamond shape of the ley lines at which point more lines from the four axes join to result in markedly increased magical power

Inner-sight: The ability to see into one's physical self and manipulate the elements present there in order to heal or change appearance

Keystone: One of four stones imbued with magical properties meant to act as a deterrent and obstacle to anyone hoping to misuse the power of the ley lines. The keystones are intended to have a dampening effect on the amount of magical power flowing to the hub and, therefore, the Great Gate.

Leighis leaf: Healing leaf

Leighis tree: A very tall tree with green leaves over most of the foliage and capped with dark red leaves at the top. All its leaves have healing properties, but the red ones are more potent.

Ley lines: Invisible lines of magic that join at four points (axes), forming the shape of a diamond. More of these lines travel from the axes to the center (the hub).

Mo grá: My love

Protectors: Those assigned the responsibility of protecting their people

Seers: A race of people of the realm of Sterrenvar who have the gift of Sight, with images of the past, present, and future coming to them in dream-visions. They are also capable of seeing into their own physical selves, an ability referred to as inner-sight.

Sight: The ability to receive images of the past, present, or future during dream-visions

Seer champions: The four seer warriors appointed as overseers and guardians of the four Gates which held the keystones. There are always four others in training to take the place of any one or any number of them if needed.

Shifters: Beings that can shift between human and animal form at will. More human than animal, their spirits and physical forms contain elements of both. They share a strong kinship with the true animal they share form with.

Snowbeast: A large animal that lives mostly in the northern mountain range of Sterrenvar called the Thuaidh Mountains. It has matted white fur, and is similar in shape to a hyena, with it's front legs slightly longer than the back, thus making the shoulders taller than the rump. On an average snowbeast, its body is as broad as a human male laying horizontal and it is twice as tall as the average human male. The snowbeast has an icy breath that can freeze a man solid in seconds. Rumor has it that they have been known to stomp their victims after freezing them, thereby shattering them.

Sterrenvar: The name of the realm in which this story is set

Acknowledgments

The writing of this book would not have been possible without the love and patience of my husband and kids. Without their support and understanding, it would have been impossible for me to fit the many hours needed for research and writing into an already busy schedule.

Thank you also to my friend Gwendoline, who acted as my sounding board and beta reader throughout this process. I know this story was improved by your input.

Many thanks to the multi-talented Aidana WillowRaven, who worked closely with me on this second edition. In her work on the cover, formatting and design, and editing, she kept an open dialogue with me, allowing my input and ideas to be incorporated in these areas as well. I am incredibly pleased with the work she has done. This book is what it is, and is exactly what I envisioned, because of her tireless work and dedication.

I also want to acknowledge to my readers that, yes, I use Celtic words and names for many of the people and places in this book and, no, they are not all used correctly. In fact, I have intentionally changed some of the words just a little bit to fit my purposes. In most cases, the names were chosen purposefully to reflect something about the personality of that character. I do not pretend to be an expert in Irish or Scottish Gaelic, and I apologize to the speakers of these languages for any mistakes. I chose to use the Celtic language as a nod to my ancestry and in honor of my mother, who loved Celtic music and lived the last three months of her life in hospice listening to as much Celtic music as we could find.

Αυτhor Biography

Sherry Leclerc holds a B.A. in English and French Language and Literature, as well as a B. Ed. As a holder of a third Dan (degree) black belt in Taekwondo, she employs her knowledge of martial arts to create realistic fight scenes in her writing.

Having left her native province of Newfoundland for the very first time when she was nineteen, she has since traveled to many different places in the world. She draws upon her various experiences help shape her writing.

A teacher by day and an avid reader and writer by night, Sherry currently lives in Ontario with her husband, two kids, and numerous pets.

Follow Sherry on Social Media:

Website:	www.sherryleclerc.com
Facebook:	https://www.facebook.com/SherryLeclercAuthor/
Twitter:	@sleclercauthor
Instagram:	@sherryleclercauthor
Google +:	https://plus.google.com/112138646094597241799
LinkedIn:	https://www.linkedin.com/in/sherry-leclerc-3235b458/

CPSIA information can be obtained
at www.ICGtesting.com
Printed in the USA
LVOW13s0749200218
567160LV00007B/12/P